MW01230736

THE DEPUTY

Paul Corricelli

dizzyemupublishing.com

DIZZY EMU PUBLISHING

1714 N McCadden Place, Hollywood, Los Angeles 90028

dizzyemupublishing.com

The Deputy
Paul Corricelli

ISBN: 9798535610672

First published in the United States
in 2021 by Dizzy Emu Publishing

Copyright © Paul Corricelli 2021

Paul Corricelli has asserted his right under the
Copyright, Designs and Patents Act 1988 to be
identified as the author of this work.

1 3 5 7 9 10 8 6 4 2

This book is sold subject to the condition that it
shall not, by way of trade or otherwise, be lent,
resold, hired out, or otherwise circulated without the
publisher's prior consent in any form of binding or
cover other than that in which it is published and
without a similar condition, including this condition,
being imposed on the subsequent purchaser.

dizzyemupublishing.com

THE DEPUTY

Paul Corricelli

THE DEPUTY

Written by

Paul Corricelli

STURM UND DRANG:

EXT. STREET - MORNING

A new day dawns over a small, forgettable town.

A Sheriff's cruiser travels at a leisurely pace down tree
lined streets, past a trailer park in various states of
disrepair.

INT. SHERIFF'S CRUISER - CONTINUOUS

DEPUTY SAM, 29, a few chicken fried steaks past svelte, hair
a little too long, with a thread bare attempt at a mustache,
drives with the window down.

A young couple is being led down the sidewalk by their canine
companion. Sam waves and calls out--

                    DEPUTY SAM
          Morning folks.

The couple clock the Deputy with a sour look and ignore the
gesture, continuing on their way.

Oblivious, Sam drives away, enjoying the morning drive.

EXT. CHURCH - MORNING

A Sheriff's cruiser is parked in front of a quaint but
unkempt church.

SHERIFF BRIMMEL, 59, a leader of men, fair but imposing,
slides out of the car, a folded piece of paper clutched in
his fist and a scowl on his face.

He throws a look to two teenagers leaning against the side of
the building and proceeds up to the front door with purpose.
He knocks and waits--

No answer. He frowns and gives the door one hard whack, then
walks around the building to the teenagers.

A boy, GIBBY, 13, and a girl, KIMMY, 14, are hudled together,
looking at Gibby's phone, unaware of the Sheriff's presence.

Kimmy pulls a few dollars out of her pocket and flips through
them.

                    KIMMY
          Text him again.

                         GIBBY
              I just did, like two seconds ago--

                         SHERIFF BRIMMEL
              Shouldn't you two be headed to
              school?

              GIBBY   KIMMY
Shit!   Jesus christ!

Gibby shoves the phone back in his pocket, nervous. Kimmy
does the same with the cash.

                         KIMMY (CONT'D)
              Yeah, we were just waiting for a
              friend.

                         GIBBY
              Guesse he's not coming, so... we're
              gonna go--

Gibby grabs Kimmy's arm and drags her away.

                         SHERIFF BRIMMEL
              Hey!

The kids stop--

                         SHERIFF BRIMMEL (CONT'D)
              C'mon, I'll give you a ride.

                         GIBBY
              No, that's cool, we like to walk...
              thanks!

They both speed-walk away.

The Sheriff throws an annoyed look to the church and walks
back to his car. He slides in and tosses the crumpled paper
onto the seat next to him.

EXT. DINER - MORNING

Two men stand in front of the local diner--

MIKEY TREMAINE, 30, a cretin, dog hater, watches his
childhood buddy, BILLY CRICKETT, 28, what he lacks in brains
he makes up for in girth, sweep the entryway.

A Sheriff's cruiser pulls up and parks. Deputy Sam climbs out
and heads to the door.

                         DEPUTY SAM
                    Morning gentlemen.

Mikey and Billy throw Sam dark looks.

                         MICKEY TREMAINE
                    Dick head.

Billy flips him the bird as he passes. Sam is, again,
oblivious.

INT. DINER - CONTINUOUS

Sheriff Brimmel sits at the counter. Sam slides onto the
stool next to him with a nod.

TREMONT TREMAINE, 56, Mikey's father, owner of the diner,
perpetually angry and looking for someone to take it out on,
stands behind the register. He gives Sam a sour look.

A waitress steps out of the kitchen with a coffee pot in hand-

SOPHIA TREMAINE, 27, Tremont's daughter, quiet-out of
necessity and, through no fault of her own, born into the
wrong family... and a female.

Sophia fills Sam's coffee cup with a genuine smile.

                         SOPHIA TREMAINE
                    Hi, Sam.

                         DEPUTY SAM
                    Beautiful sunrise this morning,
                    Sophia. You see it?

                         SOPHIA TREMAINE
                    Through the window... It's a big
                    day.

                         DEPUTY SAM
                    I suppose.

                         SOPHIA TREMAINE
                    You fella's gonna have the usual?

          DEPUTY SAM   SHERIFF BRIMMEL
Yes, please.   Sure.

She walks away with a smile. The Sheriff nudges him with an
elbow.

                              SHERIFF BRIMMEL (CONT'D)
                         She's a nice girl, Sam, and a
                         capable waitress. Don't wait too
                         long.

Sam is embarrassed.

                              DEPUTY SAM
                         Oh, gosh, we've been friends
                         forever...

Sam fidgets.

The Sheriff puts a hand on Sam's shoulder.

                              SHERIFF BRIMMEL
                         It's not an order, son. Ask her out
                         or don't, it's up to you. I'd just
                         hate to see you miss out on
                         something special.

                              DEPUTY SAM
                         Thank you, Sheriff, but I really
                         don't think Sophia sees me that
                         way.

                              SHERIFF BRIMMEL
                         I think you may be wrong about
                         that.

Sophia apears with a fresh collection of creamers for Sam.

                              SOPHIA TREMAINE
                         So... you doin' anything special
                         tonight?

Tremont watches his daughter, a scowl on his face.

                              DEPUTY SAM
                         Don't suppose I will.

                              SOPHIA TREMAINE
                         Oh... well, that's a shame.

Disappointment is etched on Sophia's face, unnoticed by Sam.

                              SOPHIA TREMAINE (CONT'D)
                         Well, I'll go check on your order.

Sophia dissapears into the kitchen.

Sheriff Brimmel pulls a large bag out from under the counter
and places it on the stool next to him. He motions to Sophia,
who's watching from the kitchen.

She steps through the door holding a slice of apple pie with a lit candle.

> SOPHIA TREMAINE (CONT'D)
> Happy Birthday, Sam!

Sophia starts to sing "Happy Birthday." Tremont, Mikey and Billy stand back and look on with contempt.

> SOPHIA TREMAINE (CONT'D)
> Happy birthday to you, happy
> birthday to you...

The Sheriff joins in and gives the men a dark look. Tremont and his boys turn and slink away.

> SOPHIA TREMAINE (CONT'D)
> Don't forget to make a wish, Sam.

Sam blows out the candle. Sheriff Brimmel pulls a box out of the bag and Sophia clears out a place for it on the counter.

> SHERIFF BRIMMEL
> Okay, Sam, not only is it your
> birthday, but it's been one year in
> the department. I think it's high
> time you represented us properly...

The Sheriff slides the box over. Sam pulls the top off and his eyes well up.

> DEPUTY SAM
> Sheriff...

Sam pulls a brand new felt campaign hat out of the box as if it's something sacred.

> DEPUTY SAM (CONT'D)
> She's a beauty.

> SHERIFF BRIMMEL
> Well, try it on, son.

Sophie truly revels in Sam's happiness and her eyes also water. Sam slips the hat on his head... a perfect fit.

> SOPHIA TREMAINE
> Wow, Sam, it's perfect.

Sam is beaming. He dabs at his eyes, then composes himself. He shakes the Sheriff's hand.

> DEPUTY SAM
> Thank you, sir. I'll cherish it.

                    SHERIFF BRIMMEL
          You're welcome, Sam. Just take good
          care of it. A quality hat like that
          is a reflection of the man who
          wears it.

                    SOPHIA TREMAINE
          It really suits you.

                    DEPUTY SAM
          Don't worry, Sheriff, I'll treat it
          with all do respect of the office
          it represents... I'll make you
          proud, sir, I promise you that. I
          believe I've found my purpose.

                    SOPHIA TREMAINE
          It really does suit you, Sam.

                    DEPUTY SAM
          Thank you, Sophia... I know it's
          not proper to wear it indoors, but
          I don't think I'm ready to take it
          off yet.

The Sheriff pats Sam on the back.

                    SHERIFF BRIMMEL
          You keep it on as long as you like.

Sophia steps away. Mikey snickers as he washes cups behind
the counter.

                    MIKEY TREMAINE
               (mumbles)
          Fuckin' idiot.

The Sheriff shoots him a look.

                    SHERIFF BRIMMEL
          You got something to say, Mikey?

                    MIKEY TREMAINE
          What, no... I didn't say anything.

The Sheriff throws Mikey a cautionary look.

Sophia returns with their breakfast. Sam stares at his
reflection in the napkin holder--

                    DEPUTY SAM
          I can't stand it, I gotta go have a
          look in the toilets mirror.

Sam struts away with a smile as the sheriff attacks his meal, sullen. Tremont slithers up and rudely shoos his daughter away. He lowers his voice.

>   TREMONT TREMAINE
>   You okay Sheriff, you've been outta
>   sorts all morning?

The Sheriff stabs a piece of meat.

>   SHERIFF BRIMMEL
>   Guess I'm just tired of suffering
>   fools.

The Sheriff stares at Tremont.

>   TREMONT TREMAINE
>   Okay, well... I'm gonna go check on
>   the kitchen. I'll leave you to your
>   meal.

>   SHERIFF BRIMMEL
>   Tell your partner I want to see the
>   both of you tonight... at the barn.

Tremont's face falls. He slinks away and takes his anger out on Sophia.

>   TREMONT TREMAINE
>   Sophia, quit standing around like a
>   Goddamn slug.

>   SOPHIA TREMAINE
>   Sorry, Daddy.

Sophie scurries over with the coffee pot. The Sheriff softens.

>   SHERIFF BRIMMEL
>   Don't pay his bluster no mind,
>   Sophia, you're doin' a fine job, as
>   always.

>   SOPHIA TREMAINE
>   Thank you, Sheriff.

The Sheriff stares at a dark bruise peeking out from underneath Sophia's uniform sleeve.

>   SOPHIA TREMAINE (CONT'D)
>   I'm so clumsy...

Sophie pulls on the sleeve. The Sheriff shoots Tremont-who's watching from the kitchen doorway, a warning look.

Tremont wilts under the Sheriff's gaze, and turns away.

Sam slides back onto his stool, a smile on his face. He runs his fingers around the brim of the hat.

>   DEPUTY SAM
>   She's a real beauty, Sheriff.

The Sheriff smiles, but there's a darkness behind his eyes.

INT. DEPUTY SAM'S HOUSE - NIGHT

Moonlight filters through gauzy curtains. The Deputy is asleep, his campaign hat lying on the dresser.

A phone on the nightstand chirps loudly in the quiet room. Deputy Sam groans and rolls over. He sleepily fumbles for the receiver, pulling it off it's cradle--

>   DEPUTY SAM
>   Hello...

EXT. TWO-lANE COUNTRY ROAD - NIGHT

The black night is ravaged by red and blue spinning lights. An ambulance and fire truck are parked on the road.

The Sheriff's cruiser is wrapped around a large tree where the road takes a sharp turn, mangled, headlights cutting through the inky blackness--

The metal hull is torn open like an animal mauled by wolves, with the Sheriff's bloody, battered body twisted in the wreckage.

A second sheriff's cruiser comes screaming down the dark road, lights flashing. It comes to a screeching halt and the door swings open--

Deputy Sam leaps out of the car. He takes a few steps and his knees give out. He falls to the ground, trying to catch his breath.

He gets to his feet and approaches the wreckage, pushing a fireman out of the way.

Sheriff Brimmel's dead eyes stare back at him. Tears run down Sam's cheeks. He backs away, horrified, and sinks to the ground, sobbing.

EXT. DEPUTY SAM'S HOUSE - MORNING

Sophia walks up the porch to the front door. Her eyes are red and puffy. She carries a small giftbag in one hand.

She knocks on the door and waits...

INT. DEPUTY SAM'S HOUSE - CONTINUOUS

The front door opens and Sophia steps inside the small, tidy home.

                    SOPHIA TREMAINE
          Sam?

No answer. She walks into the kitchen and puts the gift bag on the counter. The basement door is open--

BASEMENT

Sam sits in the dark. A massive WWI battlefield is laid out in miniature scale before him. It engulfs most of the basement, shelves packed with supplies.

A lighted display case hangs on the wall, containing a vintage Colt 1851 Navy Revolver, with a plaque that reads - "Great, Great, Granddaddy, Earnest."

This is his sanctuary.

Sophia decends the stairs and puts a hand on Sam's shoulder. He looks up at her, eyes red and raw, broken.

                    SOPHIA TREMAINE
               It's time to go, Sam.

EXT. CEMETERY - DAY

A small crowd is gathered around an open grave. Tremont, Mikey and Billy stand apart from the crowd, eyes on the Deputy.

Sam stands with Sophia. His teary eyes are locked on a photo of Sheriff Brimmel resting atop the casket.

The Priest, FATHER JANIS, 58, gun enthusiast, a heavy handed man of the cloth who leans towards a "wrath of God" approach to theology, is mid-eulogy.

                    FATHER JANIS
          Sheriff Brimmel was righteous with
          the law, and he was righteous with
          the word of the Almighty. The
          Sheriff was a hard man, but he did
          have a soft spot for societies cast-
          offs, for those less than capable
          of makin' a name for themselves on
          their own...

Father Janis throws a quick look to the Deputy.

                    FATHER JANIS (CONT'D)
          Some might consider this a
          weakness, or a failing...

Sam fidgets. Several people in the crowd are now eyeing him
as well.

                    FATHER JANIS (CONT'D)
          ... but that's a question only God
          can answer. And He will provide
          answers to us when the time is
          right. Until then we will pray for
          a brighter day and a new beginning,
          as we await God's triumphant
          return, the glorious days of his
          rapture, and the eternal, violent
          suffering of the none-believers and
          communists... Amen.

The crowd murmurs an "amen" and begin to disperse. Tremont
motions for Sophia to follow. She gives Sam an awkward hug
and joins her father.

                    FATHER JANIS (CONT'D)
          For those interested, there will be
          a small gathering at the Diner in
          remembrance of Sheriff Brimmel. All
          food and drink will be half-off
          until four o'clock.

Father Janis tucks his bible under his arm and approaches
Sam. He pulls a handkerchief out of his pocket and shoves it
in the Deputy's chest, annoyed.

                    FATHER JANIS (CONT'D)
          For God's sake, It ain't gonna help
          yer cause to be seen weeping like a
          pissy girl.

Sam does as he's told.

                          DEPUTY SAM
                You going to the Diner?

                          FATHER JANIS
                No I ain't goin' to the Diner. I've
                done all the lying I can stomach
                for one afternoon.

Father Janis snatches the handkerchief from the Deputy's hand
and walks away.

A couple of cemetery workers lower the Sheriff's casket into
the ground. It drops the last few feet and lands hard,
rattling Sam.

INT. DINER - DAY

A few funeral attendees are there. Sam sits in his spot at
the counter. Mikey sits in a booth keeping an eye on him.

Sophia steps out of the kitchen. She slides a plate of
meatloaf in front of Sam and pours him some coffee.

As she pushes the saucer closer to him, she awkwardly places
her hand on his and leaves it there.

                          SOPHIA TREMAINE
                You doin' okay, Sam?

Sophia clocks her brother watching her, and snatches her hand
away.

                          SOPHIA TREMAINE (CONT'D)
                I know how much he meant to you.

                          DEPUTY SAM
                I feel out of sorts, Sophia...
                lost. The Sheriff was like a father
                to me... a proper father.

Tremont watches from the kitchen doorway.

                          SOPHIA TREMAINE
                Don't make much senes, does it?
                Sheriff Brimmel always told me to
                take the Parker curve at a Sunday
                afternoon pace...

Sam looks stricken, eyes watering. Sophia's eyes well up.

                          SOPHIA TREMAINE (CONT'D)
                Oh goodness, I'm so sorry, I
                shouldn't...

                    DEPUTY SAM
          It's okay, I've got to come to
          terms with his passing.

Tremont and Mikey slide onto stools on either side of Sam.

                    TREMONT TREMAINE
          You got other customers, Sophia?

                    SOPHIA TREMAINE
          Yes, Daddy.

                    TREMONT TREMAINE
          Then why are you still standing
          here?

                    SOPHIA TREMAINE
          Sorry, Daddy.

Sophia slinks away.

                    TREMONT TREMAINE
          Listen Sam, I know you were fond of
          the Sheriff, but he's dead and
          buried, and as sad as that may be
          for you, this situation has farther
          reaching implications. Implications
          that are gonna effect the town and
          your own personal life.

                    DEPUTY SAM
          What do you mean?

Tremont puts a hand on the back of the Deputy's neck.

                    TREMONT TREMAINE
          See, people in this town had
          respect for the Sheriff, a healthy
          fear even, because he was a tough
          son of a bitch. But he wasn't a
          stupid man neither. If there was a
          situation that could mutually
          benefit him, he could be persuaded
          to turn the other way--

                    MIKEY TREMAINE
          Yeah, like Clearmont--

                    TREMONT TREMAINE
          Shut the fuck up, Mikey!

                    MIKEY TREMAINE
          But...

                    TREMONT TREMAINE
          You know what, go help your dim-
          whit friend buss some tables.

Mikey slinks away with his tail between wis legs. Tremont
squeezes the Deputy's neck and pulls him a little closer.

                    TREMONT TREMAINE (CONT'D)
          I'm gonna be honest with you, Sam.
          The Sheriff was the only thing
          keeping you from getting yer ass
          beat every goddamn day...

                    DEPUTY SAM
          Um--

                    TREMONT TREMAINE
          Now, we have a situation on our
          hands because, honestly, we'd just
          as soon see you gone... But we
          can't have the State sending some
          gung-ho, hard-dick lawman out here
          to fuck things up for all of us
          hard workin' citizens. People are
          just tryin' to get what they're
          owed in life, Deputy. You get what
          I'm saying?

                    DEPUTY SAM
          Not really...

Tremont squeezes a little harder, causing Sam to wince.

                    TREMONT TREMAINE
          All you gotta do is apply for the
          vacant Sheriff's position... it's
          that simple. Then you just sit back
          and relax, throw your feet up, read
          your comic books, or play with your
          toy soldiers, and let things take
          care of themselves.

                    DEPUTY SAM
          I'm not sure that's something I'm
          ready for. Honestly, I haven't
          earned--

Tremont gives him another squeeze, cutting him off.

                    TREMONT TREMAINE
          Maybe you wanna think about
          settling down, get married... you'd
          like that, right Sam?

>   DEPUTY SAM
>   I mean, eventually...

Tremont fixes him with an intense stare.

>   DEPUTY SAM (CONT'D)
>   Yes, Sir.

Tremont let's go of Sam's neck.

>   TREMONT TREMAINE
>   You don't sound so sure. Are you
>   queer, son?

>   DEPUTY SAM
>   Uh, no... Sir.

>   TREMONT TREMAINE
>   Then we're clear.

Tremont slides off of his stool and barks an order to Sophia.

>   TREMONT TREMAINE (CONT'D)
>   Sophia, get the Deputy more coffee,
>   and his lunch is on the house.

Sophia hurries over with the coffee and refills his cup. They share a sheepish look, both under the yolk of this bully.

>   TREMONT TREMAINE (CONT'D)
>   Deputy don't pay for food or drink
>   anymore. Just like we did for the
>   Sheriff.

>   DEPUTY SAM
>   Oh-ah, I appreciate it, but that's
>   not necessary. It's actually
>   against regulations.

>   TREMONT TREMAINE
>   It's not an option, son. My
>   generosity ain't up to yer
>   discretion.

>   DEPUTY SAM
>   But, the Sheriff would never--

>   TREMONT TREMAINE
>   You know, Sam, sometimes when you
>   idolize a man, you miss the things
>   that make them human.

Tremont slaps Sam on the shoulder and walks away. Sam is shaken.

INT. KITCHEN - CONTINUOUS

Mikey is waiting for his dad when he enters the kitchen.

                    MIKEY TREMAINE
          What's all that talk about gettin'
          married?

                    TREMONT TREMAINE
          That kid ain't a leader, he's a
          follower. In case he gets cold
          feet, I want another iron in the
          fire.

INT. ASSISTED LIVING HOME - DAY

Small and dingy. The kind of place where elder abuse
definitely happens and definitely goes unreported.

Sam sits across from his mother, ANNA, 62, frail, wheelchair
bound, a grey haired women who lives mostly in the fog of her
dementia.

Sam leans forward and places a hand on his mother's.

                    DEPUTY SAM
          Mamma, I've just come from Sheriff
          Brimmel's service. It was a nice
          affair, and a good number of people
          showed up to pay respects...

Sam sits back and wipes a tear from his eye.

                    DEPUTY SAM (CONT'D)
          I wanna make you proud, Mamma. And
          I wanna make the Sheriff proud,
          because I know he'd want me to do
          my best... and I know he's watching
          over me. I promised him as much...

An orderly, CARL, 48, a turd, steps up behind Anna's chair
and begins to wheel her away without a word--

                    DEPUTY SAM (CONT'D)
          Excuse me...

Carl stops and glares at the Deputy.

                    DEPUTY SAM (CONT'D)
          We were having a conversation here.

                    CARL
          One sided maybe....

Carl wheels Anna away. Several elderly patients watch the
exchange. The Deputy tries to save face.

                    DEPUTY SAM
              Well, you take care of my Mamma. I
              believe I talked her ear off enough
              for one day.

Sam slips his hat on and walks to the door when the WOMAN at
the front counter calls out and waves him over--

                    WOMAN
              Deputy!

Sam steps up to the counter. The director of the home, MONA,
50's, permanent scowl, unsympathetic to the human condition,
slides a piece of paper towards him. Sam scans it.

                    DEPUTY SAM
              This isn't right.

                    MONA
              I disagree.

                    DEPUTY SAM
              But, I'm payed up... in full. This
              number's not even right.

                    MONA
              You was gettin' a special rate,
              thanks to Sheriff Brimmel. Now,
              seein' as he's dead, that special
              rate don't apply no longer.

                    DEPUTY SAM
              That can't be right. The Sheriff
              never mentioned anything about a
              special rate... he would have
              mentioned a special rate.

                    MONA
              Well, I don't know from what the
              Sheriff told you, but this here is
              the new rate, and it's due at the
              end of the month...

Mona leans across the counter.

                    MONA (CONT'D)
              And I got no problem throwin' that
              brain rattled old bitty out on the
              street.

                    DEPUTY SAM
          Now, hold on... no one's getting
          thrown out in the street, least of
          all my Mamma. I'll think of
          something, don't you worry.

                    MONA
          Son, I'm not worried. You pay and
          she stays. You don't, her ass is in
          the goddamn street. It's as simple
          as that. Now, fuck off, I got work
          to do.

Sam takes the paper and walks out the door, dejected.

INT. CHURCH - DAY

Father Janis sits in a pew eating a sandwich, reading an old
detective novel.

Tremont walks through the front door carrying a duffle bag. A
couple of grungy teens pass him, avoiding eye contact.

Father Janis finishes the page he's on and puts the book
down.

                    FATHER JANIS
          You're late.

                    TREMONT TREMAINE
          So.

                    FATHER JANIS
          It's rude to keep a man of God
          waiting.

Tremont drops the bag on the pew next to Father Janis.

                    TREMONT TREMAINE
          Fuck off.

Father Janis smiles and stands. He takes the bag and walks,
motioning for Tremont to follow.

                    FATHER JANIS
          You talked to Sam. It went well?

                    TREMONT TREMAINE
           God only knows.

Father Janis stops.

                    FATHER JANIS
          You trying to be funny?

                    TREMONT TREMAINE
          No.

                    FATHER JANIS
          Cuz it don't suit you... and it
          ain't funny.

                    TREMONT TREMAINE
          I'm not being funny. That boy is
          dense. He listened, but he's too
          broken up over the Sheriff.

                    FATHER JANIS
          Well, it's your job to make him
          understand. Frankie's due back any
          time.

                    TREMONT TREMAINE
          Don't worry, I'll get through to
          him.

Father Janis turns and walks into his office.

EXT. JAILHOUSE - DAY

Late afternoon sunlight casts long shadows on the quiet town.

Mikey and Billy stand in the middle of the street with a late
model pickup truck stopped dead in it's tracks.

INT. JAILHOUSE - CONTINUOUS

Sam sits at his desk hovering over the assisted living bill,
his checkbook open beside him. He's oblivious to what's
happening outside his window.

                    DEPUTY SAM
          How the hell am I supposed to come
          up with this extra money?

A man walks up to the front window with a baseball bat slung
over his shoulder and peers into the jailhouse, unnoticed--

BENNY BERG, greasy hair, grungy plaid, morally lacking, the
roadmap of a hard life etched in the lines of his face.

Benny turns away and walks into the street--

EXT. JAILHOUSE - CONTINUOUS

Mikey and Billy retreat to the sidewalk.

Benny approaches the pickup truck owned by CARLA RED, 56,
missing teeth, clutching an energy drink, and TOBIAS (TOOTS)
RED, 60, bearded, with a wad of chewing tobacco under his
lower lip... hill folk... moonshiners.

The passenger door swings open and Carla tries to exit the
vehicle--

Benny kicks her door shut, on the move--

                    BENNY BERG
          Keep yer seat, Carla.

Benny walks to the drivers side and pulls the door open. He
rudely yanks Toots out of the pickup.

                    BENNY BERG (CONT'D)
          Goddamnit, Toots, you been
          delinquent. Now I'm gonna have to
          knock more-ah' yer teeth out.

Toots lets out a yelp and stumbles, but Benny keeps him
upright.

                    TOOTS RED
          Watch my hip, goddamnit!

INT. JAILHOUSE - CONTINUOUS

The commotion outside draws the Deputy out of his revery.

                    DEPUTY SAM
          Oh, balls.

Deputy grabs his campaign hat and slides it on as he hurries
through the door--

EXT. JAILHOUSE - CONTINUOUS

Benny stands over Toots, who's down on all fours with a
bloody lip.

Carla slides out of the truck with a bottle of moonshine in
one hand and her energy drink in the other.

She clumsily hurls the bottle of moonshine at Benny and
misses wildly. It smashes on the pavement.

                    CARLA RED
          You know we ain't go no money,
          Benny B! We're waitin' for our
          goddamn disability checks! Leave us
          alone!

Sam runs into the street to get between them.

                    DEPUTY SAM
          Now, just hold on a minute...
          everyone take a step back--

                    BENNY BERG
          Piss off Deputy, and crawl the fuck
          back in yer hole.

Mikey and Billy watch with amusement.

                    MIKEY TREMAINE
          Yeah, don't concern you none,
          Deputy.

                    DEPUTY SAM
          Well, it most certainly does
          concern me. Benny has clearly
          assaulted Mister Red about the
          face... By the very definition of
          the law--

                    CARLA RED
          Shut up, asshole!

Sam is taken aback.

                    BILLY CRICKETT
          Fuckin' old hag don't even want yer
          help, Deputy.

Carla turns on Billy--

                    CARLA RED
          You shut the fuck up too, Billy,
          you dick-less degenerate.

                    BILLY CRICKETT
          Fuck you, Carla, how can I be a
          degenerate if I ain't got no dick?

Billy thrusts his hips in Carla's direction and grabs a
handful of crotch--

Mikey punches Billy in the arm.

                    MIKEY TREMAINE
          Shut up, you moron.

Sam tries to gain control of the situation.

                    DEPUTY SAM
          Benny, please put the bat down and
          let's be civilized about this...

Benny swings the bat up. It stops inches from Sam's face.

                    BENNY BERG
          You wanna loose some teeth too,
          Deputy?

Sam holds his hands out where Benny can see them, and takes a
step back.

                    DEPUTY SAM
          Now, just relax, Benny... I'm not a
          threat, and I'm not reaching for my
          sidearm.

                    BENNY BERG
          You reach for yer gun, and yer
          gonna lose more than yer goddamn
          teeth.

Carla throws her head back and drains the last of the energy
drink. She wipes her chin on her sleeve, belches, and throws
the can at Benny, missing wildly again.

                    DEPUTY SAM
          Misses Red, please stop that,
          you're not helping.

Carls gives Sam the middle finger and moves to her husband.
She struggles to help him up.

                    CARLA RED
          C'mon Toots, let's get a move-on.

Benny keeps the bat pointed in Sam's face, but watches the
Red's.

                    BENNY BERG
          This ain't settled, Carla. Leave
          him be.

--Carla lets go of Toots and charges Benny at a speed that
defies her size.

--Benny swings the bat around and jabs Carls in the mouth.

--Carla recoils backwards with a yelp, her hand over her face.

                    DEPUTY SAM
          Dammit, Benny! I'm trying to
          resolve this--

Carla screeches with a mouth full of blood.

                    CARLA RED
          Son of a bitch! Deputy, shoot that
          bastard! You seen him assault me!

                    TOOTS RED
          He attacked me too!

          CARLA RED   BENNY BERG
Shut up, Toots!   Shut up, Toots!

                    MIKEY TREMAINE
          Deputy ain't gonna shoot nobody.
          He's never even pulled his gun out
          of it's holster, except for target
          practice. Ain't that right, Deputy?

There's a small crowd gathering on the sidewalk. They snicker.

                    DEPUTY SAM
          Now, that's simply not true.

An old woman, RUTH, shouts back--

                    RUTH
          It is true, you dip-shit!

Sam is flustered.

                    DEPUTY SAM
          I fail to see how - look, I just
          don't feel that guns are always the
          best... I mean, sometimes there's,
          well... look, there's absolutely no
          need for more violence here.

Benny moves closer.

                    BENNY BERG
          You're not gonna do shit, Deputy.
          In fact, yer gonna crawl go back in
          yer hole like a scared little
          rabbit and yer gonna close the
          shades and pretend like this never
          happened. Cus you don't have the
          Sheriff around to protect you no
          more.

Benny holds the bat up to Sam's face, just touching his nose.

                    BENNY BERG (CONT'D)
          Are we clear on that, Deputy, or do
          you need a sock in the mouth too?

Ruth calls out again, relishing in the moment--

                    RUTH
          What you gonna do about this mess,
          dip-shit?

Sam lowers his voice.

                    DEPUTY SAM
          Now, Benny, be reasonable. I-I'm
          the Deputy for God's sake.

                    BENNY BERG
          Ain't no way yer walkin' away the
          hero, Sam, so you best make a
          decision. You can tuck tail and
          run, or you can leave with a shit-
          load of dental bills... you got
          insurance, Deputy?

                    DEPUTY SAM
          But... I...

Benny gives him a menacing stare.

Deputy backs slowly away from Benny, hands still raised. He
turns to the small crowd and tries to save face.

                    DEPUTY SAM (CONT'D)
          Okay now folks, let's move along.
          The situation's under control...

Benny now has Toot's and Carla cornered by their truck and is
making them turn out their pockets.

Sam slowly starts to make his way toward the Jailhouse, but
the crowd's not moving.

                    RUTH
          Yer runnin' away!

                  BILLY CRICKETT
          Yeah, run and hide, dip-shit!

Billy tries to share a conspiratorial look with Ruth but
she's not having it. She scowls back at him.

Sam slinks closer to his door. He steps up onto the curb--

                  DEPUTY SAM
          Okay, let's not make the situation
          worse. Everyone return to your
          homes...

Sam turns and pulls the door open--

                  MIKEY TREMAINE
          Coward!

                    RUTH
          Yeah, you stinkin' coward!

Sam disappears into the jailhouse to mocking laughter.

INT. JAILHOUSE - CONTINUOUS

Sam stands at the window watching Benny riffle through the
Red's truck. Benny stops. He turns and stares back at the
jailhouse--

Sam slams the blinds shut.

                  DEPUTY SAM
          Crud.

He sinks into his chair, defeated.

EXT. CLEARMONT FARMS - DUSK

Several old pickup trucks are parked in front of a large,
rust colored barn. Lights are blazing and loud southern rock
blasts from within.

A raised pickup truck pulls into the lot and parks. Tremont
and his boys climb out. Mikey pulls a couple of duffle bags
out of the bed. A fourth man slides out of the cab--

FRANKIE DATHERS, 34, lanky, made of cold hard edges and a
deeply ruthless core.

Frankie lights a cigarette and a stares at the barn. A smile
spreads across his face. Tremont and the boys head inside.

INT. DINER - NIGHT

It's quiet, only a few patrons.

Sam steps inside. He sheepishly looks around before heading
to the counter. Sophia senses his trepidation.

                    SOPHIA TREMAINE
          It's okay Sam, nobodies here.

Sam pulls off his campaign hat and sits.

                    DEPUTY SAM
          I guess you heard about what
          happened?

Sophia shrugs it off.

                    SOPHIA TREMAINE
          I don't listen much to gossip.
          Usually ain't even half a truth to
          it. At least not the worst parts.

                    DEPUTY SAM
          Except in this case it was all
          worst parts, and it's all true...
          I'm afraid I didn't handle myself
          very well...

The other guests look to Sam and whisper amongst themselves,
confirming his assessment. Sophia pours him some coffee.

                    SOPHIA TREMAINE
          Don't be too hard on yourself, Sam,
          it was your first altercation
          without... well, you know, on your
          own.

                    DEPUTY SAM
          I really fouled up, Sophia. I
          wanted to handle myself like the
          Sheriff would have, but... I'm
          afraid he'd be really disappointed
          in me...

Sam leans closer.

                    DEPUTY SAM (CONT'D)
          People don't respect me, or the
          office I represent... not since the
          Sheriff passed.

                    SOPHIA TREMAINE
          Oh-I, I don't know about that, Sam.

                    DEPUTY SAM
          I'm serious. I've been told as
          much, and people are looking at me
          differently. Or, I don't know,
          maybe I'm a damn fool, maybe
          nobody's ever respected me. They
          certainly didn't when I was growing
          up.

                    SOPHIA TREMAINE
          You're not a fool, Sam... I respect
          you.

Sophia and Sam both blush.

                    DEPUTY SAM
          Thank you, Sophia. You've always a
          kind word to say... but there's
          been a shift, I can feel it. I do
          know that much... You know Mona
          over at the home?

Sophia wrinkles her nose.

                    SOPHIA TREMAINE
          I don't much care for her.

                    DEPUTY SAM
          Well, she says I was getting a
          special rate on account of the
          Sheriff. Now I've gotta come up
          with extra money for Mamma to stay.

                    SOPHIA TREMAINE
          Well that don't seem right. You
          sure she's not makin' this up out
          of her own greed?

                    DEPUTY SAM
          I don't know, but it's ultimately
          her call... I'm not sure how I'm
          gonna come up with that money. I'm
          just about at my wits end.

                    SOPHIA TREMAINE
          I'm sorry, Sam. I don't have much
          saved, but you're welcome to what's
          there.

                    DEPUTY SAM
          I appreciate the gesture, but I
          can't do that, it's not your
          burden. I'll just have to figure
          something out...

                    SOPHIA TREMAINE
          Well, I imagine the Sheriff's
          position would come with a pay
          raise... I'm sure that would help,
          wouldn't it?

Sam wipes a hand across his weary face.

                    DEPUTY SAM
          I can't... I can't wrap my head
          around that right now.

                    SOPHIA TREMAINE
          Daddy said he's got a friend over
          in Chesterfield who can rush your
          application right through. He says
          he wants to help... he''s pushing
          real hard, Sam. Real hard.

Sam's getting frazzled.

                    DEPUTY SAM
          I don't know if I'm ready for it...
          or if I deserve it. I certainly
          haven't earned it, especially in
          light of recent events. I just feel
          like I needed more time... more
          time with the Sheriff.

Sam's eyes water.

                    SOPHIA TREMAINE
          Sam--

Sophia puts her hand on his--

                    SOPHIA TREMAINE (CONT'D)
          I didn't mean to push... I don't
          wanna add to your distress.

Sophia takes her hand away and picks at her cleaning rag.

                        DEPUTY SAM
                   It's alright...

Sam studies his coffee mug.

                        DEPUTY SAM (CONT'D)
                   Sophia... do you think your daddy
                   and the Sheriff could have been
                   involved in anything illegal? Mikey
                   mentioned Clearmont Farm.

                        SOPHIA TREMAINE
                   Oh, I wouldn't know, but I can't
                   imagine the Sheriff doing anything
                   illegal... I mean, Daddy's always
                   working side jobs, but he would
                   never include me in any of his
                   business dealings. He doesn't think
                   women are smart with finances...
                   least not me.

Sam sips his coffee. He looks to the empty stool next to him -
the Sheriff's seat. He puts his cup down, more resolved.

                        DEPUTY SAM
                   I believe I'm gonna look into it...
                   I owe the Sheriff that much.

Tremont's pickup pulls into the parking lot--

                        SOPHIA TREMAINE
                   Looks like Daddy's back.

Sam throws an anxious look outside. He drains his coffee cup.

                        DEPUTY SAM
                   I better call it a night...

Sophia puts a hand on his arm to stop him.

                        SOPHIA TREMAINE
                   Sam, I need to tell you
                   something...

Sam slides his campaign hat on, eager to leave.

                        SOPHIA TREMAINE (CONT'D)
                   Frankie's on his way back to
                   town... Frankie Dathers.

Sam stops. His words lack conviction--

                        DEPUTY SAM
                   He's in jail.

> SOPHIA TREMAINE
> He's not... not anymore.

Truck doors slam and Sam's jolted into moving. Tremont is first through the door.

> TREMONT TREMAINE
> Still waiting on those Sheriff
> papers, Sam.

Sam puts his head down and walks out, shaken.

EXT. DINER - CONTINUOUS

Sam stops in his tracks, his way blocked by Mikey and Billy. He can't make eye contact.

> MIKEY TREMAINE
> On yer way to handle some more
> civil unrest, Deputy?

Sam lowers his head and walks around them. The boys snicker as they enter the diner.

INT. DINER - CONTINUOUS

Sophia wipes down the counter. She turns to find Tremont standing behind her. She tries to be strong, but her anxiety shows.

> TREMONT TREMAINE
> You told him?

> SOPHIA TREMAINE
> Yes, Daddy.

> TREMONT TREMAINE
> And?

> SOPHIA TREMAINE
> I don't think he's filled out the
> application yet. He's been awfully
> worried about his Mamma...

> TREMONT TREMAINE
> You tell Sam it's what you want for
> him?

Sophia hesitastes.

Tremont grabs her roughly by the arm.

>   TREMONT TREMAINE (CONT'D)
>   If I tell you to say something to
>   Sam, then you damn well better say
>   it. Understand?

>   SOPHIA TREMAINE
>   Yes.

Tremont releases Sophia from his vice-grip and storms off.

A forlorn Sophia silently wipes down the counter. Mikey
follows his father into the kitchen--

KITCHEN

Mikey almost collides with Tremont--

>   TREMONT TREMAINE
>   Jesus H, Mikey, watch where the
>   fuck yer at.

>   MIKEY TREMAINE
>   Sorry, Daddy... listen, why don't
>   you send me over to that little
>   turds house? I can get him to fill
>   out that application.

>   TREMONT TREMAINE
>   Don't be stupid. I want him to
>   think it's him that's making this
>   decision. And ain't no better
>   motivation for a man to do a thing
>   than pussy.

Mikey smiles, lasciviously, then it registers that Tremont
was talking about his sister.

>   MIKEY TREMAINE
>   Oh, c'mon! Why would you want that?

Billy bounds into the kitchen carrying a tub of dirty dishes.

>   BILLY CRICKETT
>   What'r we talkin' about?

>   MIKEY TREMAINE
>   For some reason we're talkin' about
>   Sophia's nethers.

>   TREMONT TREMAINE
>   You're an idiot. Better we put 'em
>   to good use before they dry up and
>   she ain't worth shit-all to us.

Billy puts the tray of dishes down.

                    BILLY CRICKETT
          I ain't never been with a real
          women... but I'd be willin' to give
          it a go if--

       TREMONT TREMAINE   MIKEY TREMAINE
Shut the fuck up, Billy!   Fuck you, Billy!

Billy throws his hands up--

                    BILLY CRICKETT
          I thought you was lookin' for
          volunteers--

                    TREMONT TREMAINE
          Billy, get the fuck outta here
          before I lodge my foot so far up
          yer ass that you choke up my
          toenails.

Billy sulks his way out of the kitchen.

                    TREMONT TREMAINE (CONT'D)
          That fuckin' boy ain't right.

INT. DEPUTY SAM'S HOUSE - NIGHT

Sam lies in bed, tossing and turning, a sheen of sweat on his
forehead--

INT. COMIC BOOK STORE - DREAM/FLASHBACK - DAY

Sam, 17, wearing a super hero t-shirt, is sorting new comic
books behind the counter. Sophia, 16 is hanging out.

                    SOPHIA TREMAINE
          I like your shirt, Sam.

Sam is self-conscious.

                    YOUNG SAM
          Thanks... My Mamma got if for me.

                    SOPHIA TREMAINE
          Well, she has good taste in super
          heroes.

Sam smiles.

The shop door opens and Frankie Dathers, 22, walks in. Sam's smile fades. Frankie eyes Sophia like a piece of meat as he addresses Sam.

> FRANKIE DATHERS
> Hey fuck-face, where's Dale?

Sam throws a furtive look to the back of the store and the closed office door.

> YOUNG SAM
> He-he's in back.

> FRANKIE DATHERS
> No he ain't, I seen him drive past
> the Tasty Freeze ten minutes ago.

> YOUNG SAM
> Oh.

Frankie moves to the counter and grabs Sam by the shirt.

> FRANKIE DATHERS
> You fuckin' lyin' to me, pussy-boy?

Sam cringes and Sophia interjects.

> SOPHIA TREMAINE
> He's not lying, Frankie. Dale
> leaves all the time without sayin'
> so.

Frankie pushes Sam back and grabs Sophia by the arm, dragging her to the office door.

> SOPHIA TREMAINE (CONT'D)
> Stop it!

Sophia rips her arm free and Frankie backhands her across the face, knocking her to the floor. He grabs her by the hair and drags her to her feet--

Sam follows--

> YOUNG SAM
> Frankie, don't, please...

Frankie whips a knife out of his pocket. Sam stops.

> FRANKIE DATHERS
> Follow me and I'll carve up her
> pretty face.

Frankie pushes the door open and shoves Sophia through, slamming it behind them. Sam is stricken.

INT. COMIC BOOK STORE OFFICE - DREAM/FLASHBACK - LATER

Sam is sitting at Dale's desk, head down, shoulders slumped, tears streaming down his face.

Sophia sits on the couch wrapped in a blanket, her hair a mess, her dress is torn. There are no tears in her eyes.

She turns to Sam.

                    SOPHIA TREMAINE
          Come sit with me, Sam.

Sam wipes his eyes and sheepishly moves to the couch. He sits with a space between them, wide enough to fit the silence.

                    YOUNG SAM
          I'm sorry I'm not stronger...

This brings a fresh wave of silent tears.

Sophia puts a hand on his shoulder and moves closer. Sam sinks into the embrace awkwardly. Victim consoling the failed savior.

INT. DEPUTY SAM'S BEDROOM - BACK TO PRESENT - NIGHT

Sam is curled up in the fetal position.

EXT. TOW YARD - MORNING

Sam stands in front of the Sheriff's ruined cruiser staring at the blood splattered interior. He's lost in grief. The Sheriff's badge is lodged in one of the dashboard gages.

With effort Sam manages to pry it lose. It's streaked in blood. He clutches it in his fist.

A torn, bloody piece of paper is stuck to the floor matt.

Sam pulls it free, careful not to rip it. All that's visible is part of a zeroxed signiture - "..rimmel," and part of an official stamp. Sam puts it in his pocket.

The attendant, KENNY, 20s, wearing a filthy coverall, steps out of the garage.

                    KENNY
          You all set, Deputy? I'm fixin' to
          junk her this afternoon.

                    DEPUTY SAM
          Yeah, I'm set.

Sam walks away.

EXT. CHURCH - DAY

Sam's cruiser pulls up to the curb. He climbs out and walks
up the steps to the front entrance. Something crunches under
his foot--

A tan wafer with a splash of color on top is cracked and
broken on the stair. Sam clocks it and keeps moving.

INT. CHURCH - CONTINUOUS

Sam pulls his hat off and sits in a pew. He closes his eyes--

A hand grabs his shoulder, startling him--

                    DEPUTY SAM
          Jesus Christ!

Father Janis hovers over him, scowling.

                    FATHER JANIS
          Watch yer language in this house,
          boy. Some of us still value the
          Word here.

                    DEPUTY SAM
          Sorry Father, you startled me... I
          was on my way to work and thought
          I'd stop by and say hello.

                    FATHER JANIS
          Since when do you just stop by?

Sam looks ready to protest, but thinks better of it.

                    DEPUTY SAM
          I... I heard Frankie might be
          headed back this way. I was
          wondering if you knew anything
          about that.

                    FATHER JANIS
          You accusing me of something?

                    DEPUTY SAM
          No, no... I just figured if anyone
          in town had heard anything...

                    FATHER JANIS
          Whatever Frankie does is Frankie's
          business, you know that. That boy
          ain't one to be constrained by
          mortal man.

                    DEPUTY SAM
          But, he should be in prison.

                    FATHER JANIS
          If he's meant to be in prison then
          I recon that's where he'll be.

                    DEPUTY SAM
          So he's not coming?

                    FATHER JANIS
          I didn't say that. If he's meant to
          be locked up, then he'll be locked
          up. If he's not locked up, then I'd
          say it's the will of God.

                    DEPUTY SAM
          How is that the will of God?

                    FATHER JANIS
          Son, everything that happens is
          God's plan. If it happens, it was
          meant to happen, and it happened by
          God's doing, good or bad. It's
          pretty easy to understand, unless
          yer a complete idiot... are you an
          idiot, Sam?

                    DEPUTY SAM
          No.

                    FATHER JANIS
          Then it's been explained.

Father Janis turns to leave--

                    DEPUTY SAM
          Father...

Father Janis turns, a scowl on his face.

                    FATHER JANIS
          I heard you got made a fool of by
          Benny Berg the other day....
                         (MORE)

                    FATHER JANIS (CONT'D)
          I'm beginning to wonder if you've
          got any balls at all.

He walks away.

Sam looks up at the giant wooden Jesus on the cross. It
stares back in judgement.

INT. CHURCH - FATHER JANIS'S ROOM - CONTINUOUS

Father Janis moves to a duffle bag on the bed, and opens it--

It's packed full of baggies filled with communion wafers,
each labeled with names like "Jet Fuel, Monkey Balls, Snake
Bite, and Ball Busters."

                    FRANKIE DATHERS (O.S.)
          He's an idiot...

The bathroom door opens and Frankie steps into the room.

                    FRANKIE DATHERS (CONT'D)
          He never did know when to let a
          thing be, did he?

Frankie picks up a bag labeled "Freak Beak."

                    FATHER JANIS
          I've got to admit, this is a
          brilliant way to move the product.
          I didn't think any of you were
          smart enough to come up with
          something like this.

                    FATHER JANIS (CONT'D)
          Fuck off, Frankie, I've got work to
          do.

Frankie tosses the baggie back into the duffle.

                    FATHER JANIS (CONT'D)
          See ya... Father.

Frankie slips out of the room to Father Janis flipping him
off.

Father Janis pulls the last baggie out of the duffle. It's
half empty. A few wafers slide out of a small hole in the
baggie.

He inspects the duffle and finds several thread bare holes in
the bottom. A wafer drops out of the bottom onto the floor.

                    FATHER JANIS (CONT'D)
          Idiots.

INT. JAILHOUSE - DAY

THOMAS AHYOKA, 63, American Indian, long hair in a ponytail,
faced lined like the map of a hard life, sweeps the floor.

Sam is at his desk, a birthday card open in his hands.

His eyes are moist. The card reads-- "Sam, it's an honor to
have you serving by my side! I'm proud to call you my Deputy!
Sheriff Brimmel."

The door chimes ring out and Sam looks up--

Frankie Dathers stands in front of him. Sam jumps to his
feet.

                    FRANKIE DATHERS
          Sit down, Sammy.

Sam sits. Frankie looks to Thomas. Thomas gives Frankie a
dark look.

                    FRANKIE DATHERS (CONT'D)
          You're done for the day, red
          skin... get out.

Thomas leans his broom by the door and walks out.

                    DEPUTY SAM
          What-what are you doing... how are
          you here?

                    FRANKIE DATHERS
          Time off for good behavior.

                    DEPUTY SAM
          That's not possible.

Frankie leans over the desk.

                    FRANKIE DATHERS
          Are you callin' me a liar, or do
          you not believe I can behave
          myself?

                    DEPUTY SAM
          Uh... neither.

                    FRANKIE DATHERS
          Either way, you can stop askin'
          around about me. I've made certain
          arrangements and I'm here to stay.

Sam reaches for the telephones receiver--

                    DEPUTY SAM
          Maybe I better call over to
          Shalton...

Sam grabs the phone but Frankie snatches the receiver out of
his hand and raises it above his head--

Sam let's out a yelp and tumbles backwards out of his chair.
He ends up in a heap on the floor. Frankie slams the receiver
back onto the cradle.

                    FRANKIE DATHERS
          Did you miss me, Sammy?

Sam peaks over the edge of the desk.

                    FRANKIE DATHERS (CONT'D)
          Sit down.

Sam does as he's told.

                    FRANKIE DATHERS (CONT'D)
          You need to stay the fuck outta my
          business.

                    DEPUTY SAM
          I'm the Deputy, Frankie,
          technically it is my--

Frankie snatches up the phone, holding it up menacingly--

Sam rears back and falls out of his chair again.

                    FRANKIE DATHERS
          What I do ain't none of yer affair.
          We clear?

                    DEPUTY SAM
               (weakly)
          Clear.

Sam makes an attempt to get back up--

                    FRANKIE DATHERS
          Stay down there, Sam. I don't want
          you thinkin' we're equal.

Sam sits back down on the floor.

Frankie pulls some papers out of his back pocket and slams them down on the table.

EXT. CLEARMONT FARMS - DAY

The usual array of junk cars are parked out front, along with the Tremaine's pickup.

INT. CLEARMONT FARMS - CONTINUOUS

The barn is filled with rows of metal tables, shelves, and drug making paraphernalia. Sections have been separated by clear plastic sheeting.

Tremont inspects the goods with Mikey and Billy. Frankie saunters in and walks straight for them, papers in hand. He slaps them down on the table.

                    FRANKIE DATHERS
          I told you I'd take care of things.

Tremont picks up the papers and inspects them.

                    TREMONT TREMAINE
          Goddammit, Frankie, I told you I
          wanted to play the Sophia angle
          first. I wanted this to be his
          decision, get him into the fold. We
          can't afford to have another
          situation here.

                    FRANKIE DATHERS
          First of all, don't fuckin' talk to
          me like that, Tremont. I came back
          here to run the business with you,
          I ain't one of yer dumb-ass yes
          men.

          BILLY CRICKETT   MIKEY TREMAINE
Hey!   Not cool, Frankie.

                    TREMONT TREMAINE
          Relax, Frankie. We're equal
          partners here--

                    FRANKIE DATHERS
          You can call us equal, but with the
          deal I made at Shalton, I'll
          definitely be pullin' in the lions
          share.

Mikey and Billy sulk.

> TREMONT TREMAINE
> We're not workin' on commission,
> Frankie. We're all doin' our part.
> Without us, you got no product to
> sell at Shalton. And gettin' Sophia
> and Sam hitched will cement the
> bond. Once he's in the fold he
> ain't likely to betray his wifes
> family.

This seams to placate Frankie.

> FRANKIE DATHERS
> Fine... I don't agree, but I'll
> play along. Ain't no reason Sophia
> and I can't still be friendly.

A leering smile is etched across his face.

> TREMONT TREMAINE
> Don't fuck up my plan, Frankie.

> FRANKIE DATHERS
> Relax, Tremont... you take care of
> the forms, I got business to attend
> to. And I told the idiot you wanted
> to see him at the diner. You can
> play yer stupid family angle....
> You're welcome.

Frankie walks away. Billy and Mikey are still sulking.
Tremont turns on them--

> TREMONT TREMAINE
> If you two don't want people to
> think yer dumb, then stop acting so
> Goddamn stupid all the time.

Tremont storms off.

INT. ASSISTED LIVING HOME - DAY

Mona sits behind the reception desk with her feet up, reading
a magazine.

Sam walks in. He pulls off his hat and approaches the
counter.

Mona is put out by the interruption. She looks up at Sam,
then her eyes return to the magazine.

                         MONA
             Yer Mamma's in the den, pretending
             to watch TV with the other
             invalids.

Sam places his hat on the counter.

                         DEPUTY SAM
             I'm not here to see my Mamma...
             well, I am, but I've got other
             business first. Now, with news of
             this new rate increase and the
             added financial burden, I'd like to
             lodge a formal complaint with--

Mona puts a hand up to stop Sam.

                         MONA
             Put it in writing and submit it to
             management.

                         DEPUTY SAM
             But, you're management.

Mona tosses her magazine on the counter, put out.

                         MONA
             That's right, I am, and I don't
             appreciate you bein' such a tight-
             ass. You're tryin' to take food
             outta my kids hungry mouths.

                         DEPUTY SAM
             You don't have kids.

                         MONA
             That ain't the fucking point now is
             it, Sam?

                         DEPUTY SAM
             What?

                         MONA
             The point is, you're a selfish son
             of a bitch.

Sam takes a step back from Mona's ire. He grabs his hat off
the counter and walks away, frustrated.

DEN - LATER

Sam sits with his mother in a quiet corner.

                         DEPUTY SAM
               I've never had a lot of friends...
               or maybe any, aside from Sophia,
               but ever since the Sheriff died
               I've been, well, I feel lost.

Sam sighs.

                         DEPUTY SAM (CONT'D)
               I won't burden you with this,
               Mamma, you were there for my
               formative years... I guess I'm just
               at a time in my life when I thought
               I'd be done with the cruelty of
               others. And I'm being pressured by
               certain people to do things that
               I'm not ready for.

Sam's mother stares blankly back at him.

                         DEPUTY SAM (CONT'D)
               Sorry, I'm rambling... I do have
               something I wanted to tell you. I
               don't want you to hear this from a
               stranger... Frankie's back--

Anna grabs Sam's hand and holds tight, startling him. She
stares him dead in the eyes and pulls him close.

                         ANNA
               You're a better man than you
               know...

Sam pulls back, tears in his eyes. Anna's face is blank
again. The moment has passed. Sam pats her hand, then stops--

                         DEPUTY SAM
               Mamma, where are your rings?

Sam is up and on the move--

ANNA'S ROOM

Sam enters his mother's room. He goes right for the dresser
and rummages through the top drawer.

He pulls out a decorative wood jewelry box and opens it--

It's empty.

                         DEPUTY SAM (CONT'D)
               Son of a bitch.

He storms out.

FRONT DESK--

Sam's face is red. He goes right to the counter. Mona is as apathetic as ever.

> DEPUTY SAM (CONT'D)
> Who else has been here to visit
> with my Mamma?

> MONA
> How the hell would I know? Lot's of
> people come through those doors.

> DEPUTY SAM
> Well, that's just not true, and
> nobody comes to visit with Mamma
> but me.

> MONA
> I guess you just answered yer own
> question then... Check the visitors
> log if you don't believe me.

Sam looks down at the book. It's pages are empty. Nobody has ever filled it out.

Sam raises his voice, possibly for the first time ever. It's not lost on Mona.

> DEPUTY SAM
> Nobody fills out this damn book and
> you know it! I'm asking you
> personally if you've seen anyone
> visit my Mamma or go into her room?

> MONA
> I have not, and don't you raise
> your voice to me--

Sam slaps his hand on the counter, startling Mona, and eliciting looks from the staff and patients.

Sam stares at Mona, his face red, pressure building. He turns and storms off.

DEN--

Sam sits across from his mother, trying to compose himself.

> DEPUTY SAM
> I'm sorry you had to witness that,
> Mamma... I'm trying to keep my
> composure, but I'm being pulled--

Carl appears out of nowhere. He grabs the handles of Anna's wheelchair and pulls her away--

                    DEPUTY SAM (CONT'D)
          What are you doing?

Carl stops.

                    CARL
          Time for her medicinals. You know
          the drill.

Sam gets up out of his chair.

                    DEPUTY SAM
          I'm in the middle of a conversation
          here, Carl!

                    CARL
          And I've got a schedule to keep.
          World don't revolve around you.

Carl turns and pushes Anna away. Sam is on the move--

Sam grabs Carl by the shoulder and pulls--

Carl holds on to the hand grips, refusing to let go.

                    CARL (CONT'D)
          What the hell are you doing?

Sam uses both hands and pries Carl's fingers off the grip.

                    DEPUTY SAM
          Get your Goddamn hands off her,
          Carl!

Carl releases his grip and puts his hands up.

                    CARL
          Jesus Christ, Sam...

Mona steps out from behind the counter.

                    MONA
          Deputy, what the hell are you
          doing?

Sam pushes Carl out of the way. He spins Anna around and wheels her back to her original resting place.

                    DEPUTY SAM
          Don't say a damn thing, Carl, just
          go about your routine...
                         (MORE)

                    DEPUTY SAM (CONT'D)
          and you better start treating my
          Mamma with the respect she
          deserves!

Carl looks to Mona who gives him a nod. He walks away, hatred
burning in his eyes.

Sam sits and wipes his sweaty palms on his trousers. He
speaks to his mother but is really addressing the room.

                    DEPUTY SAM (CONT'D)
          I won't have you disrespected
          anymore, Mamma. I won't stand for
          it!

He leans across and pats her hand.

Mona sits back down, but keeps a weary eye on the Deputy.

EXT. TWO-LANE ROAD - NIGHT

A Dodge Charger cuts through the night, it's headlights
raking across heavily wooded areas with every twist and turn.

INT. DODGE CHARGER - CONTINUOUS

Frankie sits behind the wheel, drinking a beer and smoking as
he drives. Heavy metal blasting from the stereo.

INT. DINER - TREMONT'S OFFICE - NIGHT

Sophia is sitting across from her father.

                    SOPHIA TREMAINE
          What if Sam doesn't love me, Daddy?

                    TREMONT TREMAINE
          Love? Who said anything about love?
          I don't give a good Goddamn if Sam
          loves you. This is bigger than your
          selfish desires, it's for the good
          of the family.

                    SOPHIA TREMAINE
          You mean for the good of your
          business--

Tremont backhands Sophia across the face. She recoils and
puts a hand to her stinging cheek, as tears well in her eyes.

                    TREMONT TREMAINE
          See what you make me do, Sophia?
          That's on you. I'm tryin' to help
          this family and keep us safe... to
          protect our interests. And this is
          the best way to cement our futures.
          I know you don't understand shit
          about the way the world works, but
          arranged marriages have been goin'
          on for thousands of years. It's a
          benefit to both parties. Can your
          simple mind not comprehend what I'm
          trying to do here?

Sophia pouts. She continues to stare at the floor, her hand
to her face.

                    TREMONT TREMAINE (CONT'D)
          Would you rather I pledge you to
          Frankie? Cuz that's option number
          two.

A spike of terror flashes across Sophia face. She shakes her
head - no.

                    TREMONT TREMAINE (CONT'D)
          Then stop sniveling and clean
          yourself up.

Sophia unfolds from her chair, wiping away her tears.

                    SOPHIA TREMAINE
          What if Sam doesn't want me?

                    TREMONT TREMAINE
          He will, if he knows what's good
          for him.

Sophia shuffles to the door and turns to her father.

                    SOPHIA TREMAINE
          Daddy, please don't hurt Sam...

Sophia walks out of the office. Tremont calls after her.

                    TREMONT TREMAINE
          Ain't no good ever come from lovin'
          someone... you remember that!

INT. DEPUTY SAM'S CRUISER - NIGHT

Sam drives down a dark forest lined road. Determination in
his eyes.

He has a photo of Sheriff Brimmel taped to the dashboard.

EXT. DARK ROAD - CONTINUOUS

The Sheriff's cruiser turns off the road onto a small dirt
path. It pulls up to the wood-line and parks, hidden from
view.

Sam gets out of the cruiser and takes off on foot,
disappearing into the trees.

EXT. WOODS - CONTINUOUS

Sam pulls out his flashlight and flips the switch - it
doesn't work. He runs into a low hanging branch, knocking his
hat off.

                    SAM
          Son of a...

He picks up his hat and knocks the dirt off--

INT. FRANKIE'S DODGE CHARGER - CONTINUOUS

Frankie slows the car and turns onto an a dark road--

EXT. WOOODS - NIGHT

Sam, hat in hand, pushes through thick undergrowth. He
emerges at the edge of a clearing, Clearmont Farm looming in
front of him--

Sam keeps to the shadows and slinks closer.

EXT. BARN - CONTINUOUS

Sam tries the side door, but it's locked. He moves to a
window and wipes at the grime, but the window has been
painted black from the inside.

He tries to push it open, but it doesn't budge--

INT. BARN - CONTINUOUS

Benny Berg sits in a chair with his feet up on a desk,
smoking pot from a skull bong. His eyes are slits.

A small desk lamp illuminates an open "nudie" magazine.

EXT. BARN - CONTINUOUS

Sam pulls out a pocket knife and forces the blade between the
window frame, trying to catch the lock. It passes through the
gap and an alarm shatters the silence--

INT. BARN - CONTINUOUS

Benny nearly falls out of his chair. He pulls a pistol out of
his waistband and is on the move--

EXT. BARN - CONTINUOUS

Sam takes off running. He slips on the lose dirt of the
parking lot and falls to the ground--

Several tan disks with colorful markings are lying in the
dirt. He snatches them up and scrambles to his feet, running
away as fast as he can--

The side door blasts open and Benny stumbles out, just in
time to catch a glimpse of a dark figure as it disappears
into the black woods--

EXT. WOODS - CONTINUOUS

Sam runs, winded. He stops and puts his hands on his hips,
taking deep ragged breaths. He scans the woods behind him--

All clear. He opens his hand and inspects the tan disks.

EXT. BRIGHTON CORRECTIONAL FACILITY - NIGHT

A good size prison in the middle of nowhere, threatening to
be swallowed up by the heavy woods that surround it.

Frankie's car is parked in the lot with the lights off.

INT. FRANKIE'S DODGE CHARGER - CONTINUOUS

Frankie's fingers drum the steering wheel. He checks his
watch. It's 10:30.

He finishes off the can of beer in his lap, throwing it on
the floor with several other discarded empties.

There's a knock on the passengers side window, startling him--

                         FRANKIE DATHERS
                Jesus.

A MAN is standing outside the passenger window, in shadow. He
tries the door but it's locked. Frankie rolls down the window
half-way and the man steps into the light--

Warden WILLIAM KEPLER, late 50's, with a paunch and bad tie,
pulls the collar of his jacket up to help hide his face. He
leans close, throwing a furtive look around the parking lot.

                         FRANKIE DATHERS (CONT'D)
                Hello Willie. You're looking well.

William bristles.

                         WARDEN KEPLER
                I'm not doing this through the
                window. Let me in.

                         FRANKIE DATHERS
                I don't really want you in my car,
                Willie, I just had the upholstery
                cleaned.

                         WARDEN KEPLER
                Let me in the car, Frankie. I'm the
                Goddamn Warden, I can't be seen out
                here with you.

                         FRANKIE DATHERS
                Fine.

The Warden tries the door, but it's still locked. His hand
slips of the handle from the effort.

He takes a step back and puts his hands on his hips, clearly
aggravated.

Frankie chuckles. He presses the button and the locks pop.
Warden Kepler opens the door and slides into the car, pushing
away the empty beer cans with his foot.

There's a large brown package on the seat between them and a
handgun in Frankie's lap.

                         WARDEN KEPLER
                Not funny... and stop calling me
                Willie.

                         FRANKIE DATHERS
                That's your name.

                    WARDEN KEPLER
          It certainly is not, and you know
          it. My name is William.

                    FRANKIE DATHERS
          You're such a tight-ass... William.

Frankie picks up the package and shoves it at the warden. The
warden is taken aback.

                    WARDEN KEPLER
          This is exceptionally more then was
          pre-arranged. I couldn't possibly
          move this much...

                    FRANKIE DATHERS
          You can and you will, unless you
          want the state to know you're
          running an escort service out of
          the prison. And this is just phase
          one of my plan. Pretty soon we're
          gonna expand beyond the walls of
          this shit palace.

                    WARDEN KEPLER
          Expand... are you insane?

                    FRANKIE DATHERS
          I know you run your little
          operation down in Brenton and
          Lancer. I got people on the inside,
          Willie. I know every crooked thing
          you got your hands in, and those
          are prime locations to move more
          product. I figure by the time you
          finish moving this stuff, I'll be
          ready to expand.

                    WARDEN KEPLER
          This is beneath even you Frankie. I
          included you in my... operation,
          while you were here, and you made
          quite a bit of money through me...
          and I forged your goddamn release
          papers. You could cut me a little
          slack.

                    FRANKIE DATHERS
          Ain't nothin' beneath me, Willie.

Frankie's rests his hand on top of the handgun in his lap.

                    FRANKIE DATHERS (CONT'D)
          Nothin.'

The warden stares back at him. No use arguing with this man.

                    FRANKIE DATHERS (CONT'D)
          Well... get the fuck out, Willie.

The warden slides out the car and slams the door behind him.
Frankie presses the button and rolls down the window. The
warden turns back.

                    FRANKIE DATHERS (CONT'D)
          Send one of the girls my way.

                    WARDEN KEPLER
          Fine.

                    FRANKIE DATHERS
          But not Jenny, too many fucking
          tears.

The Warden walks away, fumming.

INT. SAM'S CRUISER - NIGHT

Sam pulls up to the curb in front of his house and parks. He
studies the wafers in his hand.

He opens the glove compartment and pulls out a clear baggie
and drops them inside.

EXT. FRANKIE'S DODGE CHARGER - NIGHT

Frankie leans against the side of his car smoking, watching a
young woman approach-- KIMY, 23, her looks somewhat
diminished by the effects of heavy drug use and abusive men.

Kimy steps up and takes the joint from his hand, taking a
long drag. She has two black eyes and her nose is swollen.

                    FRANKIE DATHERS
          Hey, Kimy.

                    KIMY
          Not too rough tonight, Frankie. I
          think the last guy might'a broke my
          nose.

Her hand absently wanders up to gently caress the area.

                    FRANKIE DATHERS
          You want me to break something of
          his?

                    KIMY
          No... just don't hit me in the
          face, okay?

                    FRANKIE DATHERS
          I ain't makin' no promises.

Frankie steers her into the back seat of the car and climbs
in after her.

INT. DINER - DAY

Sam sits at his usual place at the counter, nursing his
coffee. Sophia refills his cup.

She can't make eye contact.

                    SOPHIA TREMAINE
          Sam, I'm sorry... this is Daddy's
          doing...

                    DEPUTY SAM
          What's that?

Tremont slides onto the seat next to Sam. Sophia makes a
beeline for the kitchen. It's not lost on Sam.

                    TREMONT TREMAINE
          I've decided that it's hight time
          you and Sophia got hitched.

                    DEPUTY SAM
          What?

                    TREMONT TREMAINE
          The two of you ain't getting any
          younger and I damn well don't see
          any other prospects in town for
          you. It's time to settle down, make
          some babies, put down some roots
          and join the family... that's my
          family, if my intention wasn't
          clear.

Sam is flustered.

                    DEPUTY SAM
          A baby?

                    TREMONT TREMAINE
          Son, a man don't hang around with a
          woman as much as you have without
          wanting to fuck her.

                    DEPUTY SAM
          Sir, that's your daughter...

                    TREMONT TREMAINE
          Look, I'm trying to be nice here,
          but I've made my decision... when
          you sit around too long with your
          thumb up your ass, other people
          have got to steer you in the right
          direction, and that's what I'm
          doing.

                    DEPUTY SAM
          Sir, you can't just make this kind
          of decisions for me... for us--

Tremont slaps the counter top, startling him.

                    TREMONT TREMAINE
          Jesus H Christ, I'm loosing
          patience with you, boy!

Tremont yells in the direction of the kitchen door.

                    TREMONT TREMAINE (CONT'D)
          Sophia, quit hiding behind the
          Goddamn door and come out here!

                    DEPUTY SAM
          I don't understand...

The kitchen door swings open and Sophia, mortified, slowly
makes her way to the counter.

Tremont pats the Deputy on the back.

                    TREMONT TREMAINE
          I hope I don't need to say this,
          but no funny business until you two
          are wed. You keep yer hands out of
          her pants, for now.

                    DEPUTY SAM
          Sir, I didn't agree to anything...

Tremont's cellphone rings and he walks away to answers it.

                    SOPHIA TREMAINE
          Sam... I just want you to know, I,
          I didn't put daddy up to this.

                    DEPUTY SAM
          You deserve better than this.

Sophia puts her hand on top of Sam's.

                    SOPHIA TREMAINE
          Sam... Daddy may be forcing this on
          me, but--

                    DEPUTY SAM
          You deserve better...

A few customers come in and sit at the counter near Sam,
making him more self conscious.

                    SOPHIA TREMAINE
          Sam, you don't understand...

                    DEPUTY SAM
          No, I don't suppose I do.

Sophia lowers her voice.

                    SOPHIA TREMAINE
          Why don't you come back tomorrow at
          closing. I'll make you dinner and
          we can talk in private.

                    DEPUTY SAM
          Okay... that'd be nice.

Sam gets up from his seat, confused. He walks out of the
diner in a daze.

INT. PRISON - WARDEN KEPLER'S OFFICE - DAY

Warden Kepler sits at his desk, frazzled. A giant of a man
sits across from him--

Officer KENT FISK, made of hard bark and few words. He's
known simply as, Mister Fisk.

                    MISTER FISK
          It's not impossible, boss, I can
          move the merchandise.

                    WARDEN KEPLER
          That's not the point. Frankie's out
          of control, he's reveling at having
          control over me, and I won't have
          it. I mean to put an end to this
          before that animal gets us all
          locked up.

                    MISTER FISK
          You want me to handle it?

                    WARDEN KEPLER
          No, we can't take a chance that
          someone might connect you with
          this...

Warden Kepler taps a manila folder sitting on his desk.

                    WARDEN KEPLER (CONT'D)
          Did you check on Jimmy Grimes
          condition?

                    MISTER FISK
          Yeah, the Doc says he's recovering
          from his stab wounds. Already up
          and about.

                    WARDEN KEPLER
          And his mental condition?

                    MISTER FISK
          Says he's gonna shoves his arm up
          Frankie's ass and rip out his
          guts... he doesn't know Frankie's
          gone.

                    WARDEN KEPLER
          Good... I want to see him tomorrow
          morning.

                    MISTER FISK
          I'll make it happen.

The big man walks out the door and lumbers down the hallway.

EXT. CLEARMONT FARMS - DAY

Frankie and Tremont inspect the window.

                    TREMONT TREMAINE
          Window seems fine. I'll have one of
          the boys reconnect the sensor.

                    FRANKIE DATHERS
          How the fuck did Sam find out about
          this, Tremont?

                    TREMONT TREMAINE
          You're sure it was him?

                    FRANKIE DATHERS
          Benny said he was carrying that
          Goddamn hat...
                    (MORE)

                    FRANKIE DATHERS (CONT'D)
          And he runs like a fucking girl.
          Now, how the fuck did he find out
          about this place?

                    TREMONT TREMAINE
          Mikey might 'ah mentioned the
          name... Fuck. Well, guess I better
          speed things up.

Frankie lights a cigarette, a rye smile on his face.

                    TREMONT TREMAINE (CONT'D)
          What the fuck are you smiling
          about.

                    FRANKIE DATHERS
          Pushing Sam's button's.

                    TREMONT TREMAINE
          Listen, Frankie, the idea is to
          control the situation, not break
          him.

Frankie's mood turns on a dime. He throws his cigarette on
the ground and stamps it out angrily--

                    FRANKIE DATHERS
          Maybe you should stop worrying
          about what I'm doing and
          concentrate on you and your idiot
          boy not fucking this whole thing
          up!

Frankie storms off.

INT. JAILHOUSE - DAY

The setting sun paints the world outside the windows in red
and gold. Sam sits slumped in his chair in the fadding light.

A new bulletin board is hung on the wall with a collage of
afirmations, cut out from books and magazines.

Sam sits at his desk while Thomas Ahyoka sweeps the floor.
Sheriff Brimmel's badge-freshly cleaned, is sitting on top of
a photo of Sam and the Sheriff.

                    THOMAS AHYOKA
          You still with us, Deputy?

                    DEPUTY SAM
          Mmm...

                    THOMAS AHYOKA
          Just that you haven't moved a
          muscle in nearly an hour... don't
          think you even blinked but once.

Sam sighs, his eyes puffy and red.

Thomas shufles to a desk lamp and moves to turn it on--

                    DEPUTY SAM
          Please don't.

Thomas pulls his hand away.

                    DEPUTY SAM (CONT'D)
          Sheriff used to stop and watch the
          sunset every day... said it's a
          time for reflecting on the good
          deeds on the day, and weighing your
          involvment.

                    THOMAS AHYOKA
          That's an old Indian saying.

                    DEPUTY SAM
          Is it?

Thomas scratches his stubbly chin.

                    THOMAS AHYOKA
          Don't know... but it should be.

Sam nods in agreement.

                    DEPUTY SAM
          I don't know if I can do it, Mister
          Ahyoka.

                    THOMAS AHYOKA
          Sure you can. Just come stand by
          the window.

                    DEPUTY SAM
          Not that... this, trying to fill
          the Sheriff's shoes. I'm not the
          man he was.

                    THOMAS AHYOKA
          Don't see as you can be...

Thomas resumes his sweeping, off of Sam's hurt look.

                              THOMAS AHYOKA (CONT'D)
                    You can't be who the Sheriff was,
                    you got to be who he wanted you to
                    become... Sheriff wasn't one to
                    waist time. Don't think he would'a
                    picked you for his Deputy if he
                    didn't see something in you the
                    rest of us didn't.

Sam nods. He takes the badge and locks it in the top desk
drawer. He takes the photo to the bulletin board and pins it
in the center.

EXT. HOUSE - DUSK

A DARK FIGURE dressed in all black jimmies the lock on a
woodfame window with a knife. The lock slides open and the
dark figure pushes the window open.

INT. DINER - NIGHT

The place is closed, only a few lights burning for romantic
effect. Sam and Sophia sit across from one another in a
booth, both uncomfortable.

                         DEPUTY SAM
                    Sorry, this isn't much of a first
                    date, I guess.

                         SOPHIA TREMAINE
                    It was me that asked you.

Sam's embarrassed.

                         DEPUTY SAM
                    Oh... right. Sorry.

                         SOPHIA TREMAINE
                    Don't be. I just thought we should
                    talk a bit. I know we've been
                    friends for forever...

                         DEPUTY SAM
                    Sophia, It's not right. I can't let
                    you get forced into this.

                         SOPHIA TREMAINE
                    Oh.

                    DEPUTY SAM
          Your daddy basically told me I
          don't have a choice, but, I can't
          bear to hurt you, even if it means
          crossing Tremont.

Sophia's reply is barely more than a whisper.

                    SOPHIA TREMAINE
          So... you want to get out of it?

                    DEPUTY SAM
          There's something funny going on
          here, and I'm gonna get to the
          bottom of it. Tremont is trying to
          steer me towards something, I just
          don't know what that is, and
          there's something I found out at
          the farm...

Sam pulls the baggie of wafers from his pocket and lays it on
the table--

Sophia is silently crying.

                    DEPUTY SAM (CONT'D)
          Sophia, what's wrong?

Sophia wipes away the tears, frustrated. She tries to compose
herself.

                    SOPHIA TREMAINE
          Just forget it, Sam... I'll tell
          daddy you won't have me... I'll
          deal with the consequences.

                    DEPUTY SAM
          What consequences?

                    SOPHIA TREMAINE
          Daddy intends on me marrying you...
          or Frankie.

                    DEPUTY SAM
          No! I won't let that happen--

Sophia places a hand on Sam's.

                    SOPHIA TREMAINE
          I won't let that happen either...
          I'll run. I just hoped-I don't
          know, we've known each other for so
          long...

                         DEPUTY SAM
                    Do you actually want this?

Sophia abruptly slides out of the booth and stands--

                         SOPHIA TREMAINE
                    Daddy's right, you are stupid...

She snatches her cup off the table and moves behind the
counter to pour herself more coffee, and hide fresh tears.

Sam snatches up the baggie and follows, wounded.

                         DEPUTY SAM
                    Sophia.... T'm sorry

Sophia finds her voice.

                         SOPHIA TREMAINE
                    I've been closer to you than anyone
                    else in my entire life, since we
                    were ten-years-old, and I'd be
                    willing to bet you'd say the same.

                         DEPUTY SAM
                    I would... of course I would.

                         SOPHIA TREMAINE
                    You think I don't see you watching
                    me when you think I'm not looking?
                    I've been waiting and waiting for
                    years for you to work up the nerve
                    to tell me how you feel...

Sophia puts her coffee cup on the counter and looks Sam dead
in the eye.

                         SOPHIA TREMAINE (CONT'D)
                    You tell me right now how you feel
                    about me, Sam... from the bottom of
                    your heart. Or you and I are no
                    longer friends. I mean it.

Sam stares at the counter top just long enough for Sophia to
get nervous.

                         DEPUTY SAM
                    Sophia... I... I cherish our
                    friendship, more than you know...

Sophia's turn to study the counter top.

                    DEPUTY SAM (CONT'D)
          The truth is... I've never had much
          in the way of confidence, and I've
          never been very sure of anything in
          my life... but, I do know one
          thing... I... I've been in love
          with you for as long as I can
          remember.

                    SOPHIA TREMAINE
          Oh, Sam....

Fresh tears. Sophia's hands find Sam's on the counter.

                    SOPHIA TREMAINE (CONT'D)
          We're both idiots. Here we've been
          feeling the same way about each
          other for years and both too afraid
          to say it.

                    DEPUTY SAM
          Really?

Sophia nods-YES. Sam's smile fades.

                    DEPUTY SAM (CONT'D)
          But, the comic book store... I let
          that happen. I couldn't protect
          you... I didn't protect you.

                    SOPHIA TREMAINE
          Sam, that wasn't your fault.
          There's nothing you could have done
          to prevent that... You know its
          true.

Sam has tears in his eyes.

                    SOPHIA TREMAINE (CONT'D)
          Have you been carrying that guilt
          with you all these years?

Sam nods-YES.

                    SOPHIA TREMAINE (CONT'D)
          Oh, Sam, I never ever blamed you
          for that. That's the past, and the
          past don't serve anyone. We need to
          focus on right now.

                    DEPUTY SAM
          Then... what do we do?

                    SOPHIA TREMAINE
                You could kiss me.

Sam stands and they both lean across the counter. Their lips
meet. Their first kiss.

INT. SAM'S HOUSE - KITCHEN - NIGHT

Sam stands in front of an open refrigerator in a pair of
sweatpants and t-shirt. He pulls out a can of soda.

Sophia's gift bag is still sitting on the counter. Sam pulls
out a replica British Mark V tank. Sam admires it.

                    DEPUTY SAM
                Oh my gosh... this is amazing.

Excited, he pulls the basement key from a drawer and freezes--

The basement door is ajar, lock busted. Sam yanks the door
open and flies down the stairs.

BASEMENT--

Sam reaches the bottom of the stairs and stops. His giant
battlefield is completely destroyed. The display case housing
the Colt 1851 is smashed, pistol gone.

Sam sinks to his knees, weeping.

INT. PRISON - WARDEN KEPLER'S OFFICE - DAY

Warden Kepler sits behind his desk, arms crossed, studying
the man seated across from him--

JIMMY GRIMES, late 30's, greasy hair pulled back in a ratty
ponytail, sits slouched in his chair, aggitatd.

Mister Fisk stands in the corner keeping a watchful eye on
the inmate.

                    JIMMY GRIMES
                That son of a bitch stabbed me and
                you set him free?

                    WARDEN KEPLER
                It was your word against his...
                besides, you seem to be doing quite
                well now.

                    JIMMY GRIMES
          That's bullshit and you know it.
          And my current condition's not a
          factor in determining his guilt.

                    WARDEN KEPLER
          Well then, perhaps you'd like a
          shot at retribution?

Jimmy sits up straighter, not what he was expecting.

                    JIMMY GRIMES
          Yes, Sir... I would.

Warden Kepler smiles.

INT. DINER - DAY

Sophia wipes down the counter, her attention on the parking
lot. Sam stands beside his cruiser staring at the ground as
if frozen in time.

Tremont appears next to her.

                    TREMONT TREMAINE
          What's he doing?

                    SOPHIA TREMAINE
          I don't know, he's been like that
          for the past five minutes.

                    TREMONT TREMAINE
          Christ.

Tremont walks away shaking his head. The door chimes sound
and Sam steps through the door looking frazzled.

                    SOPHIA TREMAINE
          Sam, what's wrong? You've been
          outside starin' at your feet.

Sam drops onto his usual stool.

                    DEPUTY SAM
          There was a break-in...
          everything's ruined, my basement
          was destroyed.

                    SOPHIA TREMAINE
          Oh Sam, no...

                    DEPUTY SAM
          And my great, great granddaddy's
          pistol was taken.

Sophia puts a hand on his.

                    SOPHIA TREMAINE
          I'm so sorry.... Who would do such
          an awful thing?

Tremont bursts through the kitchen doors holding an envelope
and wearing a ridiculous grin.

                    TREMONT TREMAINE
          Sam, great news!

                    SOPHIA TREMAINE
          Daddy, someone broke into Sam's
          house last night. They smashed up
          his basement.

                    TREMONT TREMAINE
          Oh Jesus, what, did they steal some
          of yer toy soldiers?

                    SOPHIA TREMAINE
          Daddy!

                    DEPUTY SAM
          Sir, that was my passion. I won an
          award from Battlefield Replica
          magazine...

                    TREMONT TREMAINE
          No way that's a real thing.

                    SOPHIA TREMAINE
          It is too, Daddy, and they stole
          his Great, Great, Granddaddy's
          pistol.

Tremont is losing his patients---

                    TREMONT TREMAINE
          Okay, okay, listen... I've got
          something here that's gonna make
          you forget all about your stolen
          dolls and rusty old pistol...

                    DEPUTY SAM
          Sir, that pistol was in pristine
          working condition, and it was
          passed down to me from--

Tremont slaps the envelope down on the counter.

> TREMONT TREMAINE
> Open it!

Sam reluctantly picks up the envelope - it's been opened and partially taped back together.

He pulls out a sheaf of paper and silently reads--

> DEPUTY SAM
> Sir, there's no way this could have
> happened so fast. There's a
> process, a vetting period, a-uh...
> a process.

Tremont produces another envelope from behind his back. He rips it open and pours the content on the counter--

A brand new Sheriff's badge and I.D.

> TREMONT TREMAINE
> I told you I had friends who could
> help this along.

Tremont pushes the badge to him. Sam stares at it.

> DEPUTY SAM
> This isn't right...

Tremont jabs his hand at him--

> TREMONT TREMAINE
> Congratulations, Sheriff.

Sam angrily shoves the badge and papers across the counter at Tremont and gets to his feet.

> DEPUTY SAM
> No. I didn't earn this... it's not
> right.

> TREMONT TREMAINE
> You listen to me, Sam--

> DEPUTY SAM
> No! I'm not gonna accept that until
> I've earned it!

Sam grabs his campaign hat and rushes out of the diner. Tremont throws Sophia a sour look.

EXT. HOUSE - DAY

Jimmy Grimes jumps a fence into the back yard of a small dilapidated home. He creeps to a back door and smashes out a square of glass. Reaching inside, he unlocks the door.

INT. JAILHOUSE - DAY

Sam sits at his desk, the baggie of wafers laid out in front of him. The door opens and Sophia, in a second hand white dress, and Tremont, step inside--

Sam snatches up the baggie and shoves it in his pocket, jumping to his feet.

>   DEPUTY SAM
>   What-What's happening?

>   TREMONT TREMAINE
>   Why do you always look so fucking
>   nervous, Sam?

Tremont moves to Sam's bulletin board. He frowns as he studies the sayings plastered everywhere. He reads aloud--

>   TREMONT TREMAINE (CONT'D)
>   " Positive thoughts and
>   affirmations...I have people who
>   love and respect me"- are you
>   fucking kidding me with this shit?

>   SOPHIA TREMAINE
>   Daddy!

>   TREMONT TREMAINE
>   (mumbles)
>   Jesus Christ...

Tremont moves to the front window and looks out. Sam notices Sophia's dress.

>   DEPUTY SAM
>   You look very pretty, Sophia.

>   SOPHIA TREMAINE
>   Thank you, Sam.

>   TREMONT TREMAINE
>   Put your tie on, son.

>   DEPUTY SAM
>   What's that?

Tremont moves to the door and pulls it open.

> TREMONT TREMAINE
> Put your fucking tie on.

A large man in shirt sleeves, ROY, enters carrying a
briefcase. He moves to an empty desk with a curt nod hello,
and pulls out some papers.

> SOPHIA TREMAINE
> I'm sorry, Sam, I didn't know this
> was going to happen so fast--

> TREMONT TREMAINE
> Knock it off, Sophia. It ain't too
> late for me to promise you to
> Frankie. Is that what you want?

> DEPUTY SAM
> No! No, that's not what we want.

Sophia smiles at Sam as he pulls his tie out of his desk
drawer and clips it on.

> ROY
> I've got the papers in order,
> Mister Tremaine.

Sam takes Sophia's hand.

> DEPUTY SAM
> Are we getting married right now?

> SOPHIA TREMAINE
> I wanted to call and tell you, but--

> TREMONT TREMAINE
> Get the rings out, Sophia, let's
> get this thing moving.

Sophia pulls out a wedding ring and a gold band.

> SOPHIA TREMAINE
> This is my Mamma's ring.

She hands it to Sam, and shows him the band.

> SOPHIA TREMAINE (CONT'D)
> We stopped in town to pick this up
> on the way.

Tremont takes the papers from Roy. He slaps them down on
Sam's desk and hands Sam a pen.

                         TREMONT TREMAINE
               If you two want a proper ceremony,
               you can work it out on your own and
               pay for it yourselves.

Sam and Sophia sign the documents. Tremont snatches them up
and passes them to Roy, who signs as well and shoves them
back into his briefcase.

Tremont hands Roy some cash and ushers him out. Sam slips the
ring on sophia's finger and she does the same for him. They
kiss.

                         TREMONT TREMAINE (CONT'D)
               Sophia, you can have the rest of
               the day off for your honeymoon.

Tremont shakes Sam's hand and pulls him close--

                         TREMONT TREMAINE (CONT'D)
               Don't fuck this up, Sam. You're
               part of the family now. My family.
               Everything you do reflects on all
               of us... remember that... and don't
               you ever disrespect me again like
               you did at the Diner. I'll be
               expecting you to come pick up your
               badge.

Tremont walks out, slamming the door behind him.

Sophia pulls Sam close and kisses him.

                         SOPHIA DATHERS
               I love you, Sam.

Sam's phone rings--

INT. HOSPITAL - NIGHT

Sam and Sophia burst through the front door and run to the
nurses station--

A nurse, MARY-ANN, 50s, is startled and drops a folder she's
carrying. The papers scatter across the floor.

                         DEPUTY SAM
               Where's my Mamma?

                         NURSE MARY-ANN
               Goddammit Sam, look at the mess you
               caused!

Mary-Ann begins collecting the papers.

                    DEPUTY SAM
           For God's sake.

Sam bolts past the nurses station pulling Sophia along with
him--

HALLWAY

Sam and Sophia speed-walk down the hallway. Sam calls out--

                    DEPUTY SAM (CONT'D)
           Mamma?... Mamma?

Doctor SHERMAN CUTTER, 58, steps out of a room--

                    DOCTOR CUTTER
           Sam... shush. I got patients trying
           to rest. I certainly don't
           appreciate you stressing everyone
           out. Now take a deep breath--

Sam does as he's told.

                    DEPUTY SAM
           I'm sorry, doctor Cutter, we got a
           message that my Mamma was admitted.

Doctor Cutter puts a hand on Sam's shoulder and squeezes. A
gesture of reassurance, but comes across as creepy.

                    DOCTOR CUTTER
           Relax, Sam, your Mamma's sleeping.

                    SOPHIA
           So she's alright?

                    DOCTOR CUTTER
           Well, okay, she's not exactly
           sleeping...

The doctor directs Sam and Sophia into a room--

Sam's mother is lying in bed, connected to a tangle of tubes
and wires. They stop in their tracks.

                    DOCTOR CUTTER (CONT'D)
           She's in a coma.

Sam and Sophia move to his mother's bedside. Sam takes her
hand.

                    DEPUTY SAM
          My god, what happened?

                    DOCTOR CUTTER
          It appears she may have...
               (clears his throat)
          Well-uh, she overdosed.

                    DEPUTY SAM
          Overdosed? On what?

Doctor Cutter checks his chart.

                    DOCTOR CUTTER
          Well, we're not entirely sure yet,
          we're waiting on the lab work.
          Apparently she vomited all over
          herself--

                    SOPHIA
          Doctor Cutter!

                    DOCTOR CUTTER
          Oh-sorry, you probably didn't need
          to know that... We think it might
          have been a suicide attempt.

                    DEPUTY SAM
          My Mother was a deeply religious
          woman. There's no way she would
          have done that.

                    DOCTOR CUTTER
          Hm, well, there's that to consider,
          I guess. Mona-she's who called it
          in, found some broken crackers near
          her body on the floor... found some
          in the-uh... vomit, as well.

Sam sinks into a chair next to the bed, his breathing
labored.

                    SOPHIA
          Is she gonna be alright?

                    DOCTOR CUTTER
          I'm not gonna lie to you, I just
          don't know at this point.

Sam holds his mother's hand, tears spilling from his eyes.

> DOCTOR CUTTER (CONT'D)
> (mumbles)
> Don't like tears... I'll give you
> some space.

Doctor Cutter walks out.

Sam looks to Sophia. There's a fire in his eyes--

EXT. CHURCH - DAY

The Sheriff's cruiser pulls up to the curb fast, and skids to
a stop. Sam slides out of the car and walks up the church
steps with purpose.

INT. CHURCH - CONTINUOUS

The building is quiet, just a single man sitting in the last
row of pews. He stares vacantly at the ceiling.

Sam walks past the alter to the office doors. He knocks... no
answer. He tries the handle but it's locked.

He jerks the handle up with force and it pops open--

INT. FATHER JANIS' OFFICE - CONTINUOUS

Sam closes the door behind him. He stops in his tracks--

Rows of baggies line a table against the wall, filled with
colorfully stamped communion wafers. Sam moves to the table
and opens a baggie--

The door slams behind him and Sam nearly jumps out of his
skin.

> FATHER JANIS (O.S.)
> What the hell are you doing in
> here?

Sam spins, clutching the wafers. Father Janis steps forward
and slaps them out of his hand.

> FATHER JANIS (CONT'D)
> Put those down you damn fool! Those
> are sacred, get your Goddamn filthy
> hands off them!

                        DEPUTY SAM
              These are most certainly not
              sacred. I know what these are, and
              I know what you did to my Mamma!

Father Janis lashes out, backhanding Sam across the face--

Sam staggers back against the table. Before he can recover,
Father Janis is on him with another backhand--

                        FATHER JANIS
              You little turd! Everything you
              touch turns sour! We handed you the
              Sheriff's job and you threw it back
              in Tremont's face!

                        DEPUTY SAM
              I didn't earn that!

He slaps Sam again, forcing him back into the wall. Father
Janis moves in--

                        FATHER JANIS
              You never earned a goddamn thing in
              your life. You think you're gonna
              finally grow some balls and come
              screw up my business?

Father Janis has Sam pinned to the wall.

                        DEPUTY SAM
              Stop it... stop it, Father!

Father Janis laughs--

                        FATHER JANIS
              You idiot, you keep this shit up
              and you're gonna end up just like
              your precious Sheriff.

                        DEPUTY SAM
              What-what did you do?

Father Janis grabs a handful of wafers and shoves them in
Sam's mouth, clamping his hand over his face--

                        FATHER JANIS
              Sometimes people don't know when to
              close their mouths, so they got to
              be closed for 'em!

Sam pushes his hand off, gagging, and tries to spit the
wafers out--

                    DEPUTY SAM
              Stop it... Father! Please...

Father Janis attacks again, but Sam blocks the backhand and
pushes him away, coughing and spitting out more wafers, tears
running down his face--

                    DEPUTY SAM (CONT'D)
              Daddy, stop!

Father Janis freezes, his anger turning to icy murderous
intent.

                    FATHER JANIS
              Don't you dare...

Sam pleads.

                    DEPUTY SAM
              Daddy... please...

                    FATHER JANIS
              Don't you call me that, you
              understand? I gave you up you
              worthless shit. You and your
              Goddamn mother!

Sam is unsteady, swaying, having ingested some of the drugs.
He backs away from his father's anger.

                    DEPUTY SAM
              You beat Mamma into a coma--

Father Janis attacks, smacking Sam about the face--

                    DEPUTY SAM (CONT'D)
              Stop!

Sam throws his father away from him with all his strength--

Father Janis flies into the wafer table and the whole thing
collapses, wafers scattering everywhere.

Sam backs away, trying to catch his breath.

                    FATHER JANIS
              You son of a bitch!

Sam turns and runs out of the church, crashing into pews and
stumbling his way out.

EXT. CHURCH - CONTINUOUS

Sam runs onto the front lawn and drops to his knees, trying
to catch his breath. He looks around disorientated.

                    DEPUTY SAM
          My head... so... heavy...

A few townsfolk walk by--

                    DEPUTY SAM (CONT'D)
          Help me...

They scurry away. Sam tries to get up but falls back to the
ground--

INT. HOME - FLASHBACK - NIGHT

A lamp is overturned, casting crazy shadows on the scene.
Father Janis has his wife, ANNA DATHER'S in a vice grip. He
slaps her--

Sam, 14, eye swollen, split lip, tries to pull Father Janis
off his mother and gets pushed away--

Father Janis backhands Anna and she falls back, slamming her
head against the coffee table. She lies unmoving on the
floor.

Father Janis throws a beer bottle at her and storms off,
grabbing Sam by the face and pushing him to the floor as he
passes--

There's an older boy standing in the shadows watching, a
smile on his face--

EXT. CHURCH - BACK TO PRESENT - DAY

Sam gets to his feet and stumbles away, leaving his cruiser
behind.

INT. PRISON - WARDEN'S OFFICE - DAY

Mister Fisk sits across from Warden Kepler, who is nervously
drumming his fingers on his desk.

                    WARDEN KEPLER
          He's not responding, Mister Fisk.
          Something's amiss. He should have
          reported in last night.

Mister Fisk pulls his large frame out of the chair.

                    MISTER FISK
          How do you want me to play this?

                    WARDEN KEPLER
          Avoid that idiot Deputy. In fact,
          avoid everyone. If you can pin it
          on Jimmy, great. If not, I'll leave
          it up to your discretion, just make
          sure it can't be traced back to
          us... unless you fancy being a
          resident here?

                    MISTER FISK
          Got it.

Mister Fisk lumbers away.

INT. DILAPIDATED HOUSE - DAY

Jimmy is enveloped by a ratty recliner, feet up, beer in
hand, watching TV.

EXT. PIGGLY WIGGLY - DAY

Sam sits on the ground next to a cart return rack in the
parking lot, his campaign hat laid out on discarded shopping
bags to keep it off the ground.

He's sweaty and untucked. A couple empty water bottles litter
the ground.

A souped-up muscle car rumbles past him and parks. Benny and
Frankie climb out and approach Sam.

They stand close, casting long shadows over him.

                    BENNY BERG
          I heard you had a little run in
          with yer daddy?

                    FRANKIE DATHERS
          Real Daddy, not your dead cunt
          Sheriff daddy.

                    DEPUTY SAM
          Leave me alone, Frankie, I don't
          feel good.

                    FRANKIE DATHERS
          Now you know I was never very good
          at that.

                    DEPUTY SAM
          He drugged me.

                    BENNY BERG
          Well you was snoopin' where you
          shouldn't 'ah been.

                    DEPUTY SAM
          I know what's going on at the farm.

                    FRANKIE DATHERS
          Good, then I'll make this real
          simple for you, Sammy. Forget all
          about the church, and Daddy, and
          the business we're workin' with
          Tremont, or something bad could
          hapen to you too... or maybe I pay
          a little visit to your pretty new
          bride.

Sam clenches his jaw and his fists--

                    DEPUTY SAM
          You leave Sophia alone.

                    FRANKIE DATHERS
          What's wrong Sammy, you don't want
          to share your toys with your big
          brother?

                    DEPUTY SAM
          Don't you dare touch her... Stop
          pushing me, Frankie--

Frankie takes a step closer and plants his foot on top of
Sam's campaign hat, crushing it.

                    FRANKIE DATHERS
          I ain't even begun to push you,
          Sammy.

Sam is visibly shaking. He pushes Frankie's foot away--

                    DEPUTY SAM
          Get off of my hat!

Sam snatches up the hat, pushing it back into shape.

                         DEPUTY SAM (CONT'D)
                    I swear to God, stop pushing me,
                    Frankie... if you touch Sophia...

Sam lurches to his feet--

Benny takes a step back. His jacket opens just enough to
reveal the handle of Sam's Colt revolver sticking out of his
waistband--

Sam see's it. He's strung like a piano wire... a rubber band
stretched to it's breaking point.

                         DEPUTY SAM (CONT'D)
                    My pistol... you stole my pistol!

Benny laughs and pulls his jacket back, reveling in the
moment. He puts his hand on the hilt--

                         BENNY BERG
                    This here is my gun, Sam. My great,
                    great grand-pappy give me this here
                    pistola...

Benny starts to pull the gun out of his waistband--

Sam's gun is suddenly in his hand. He pulls the trigger and a
bullet rips through Benny's face with an ear shattering blast-

Benny drops dead at Frankies feet.

Sam is almost as shocked as Frankie. He stumbles back, then
moves in for a closer look--

                         DEPUTY SAM
                    Oh God...

                         FRANKIE DATHERS
                    You son of a bitch, you fucking
                    shot him!

Sam turns in circles, confused. He spots his hat on the
ground and snatches it up, placing it on his head. He pulls
the Colt revolver from Benny's dead hand.

                         SHERIFF SAM
                    He threatened me...

Sam pushes past Frankie.

                         FRANKIE DATHERS
                    You can't just shoot him in the
                    fucking face!

Sam stops and turns back to his brother. He wipes at the tears on his face and regains his composure.

>   DEPUTY SAM
>   I-I can... he threatened me... and
>   I'm the law!

Sam turns and storms off.

INT. DINER - DAY

Late afternoon sun paints the Diner in a golden light. A few customers eat at the counter, with Sophia serving.

The kitchen doors blast open and Tremont erupts from the kitchen, red faced. Mikey follows close behind.

He makes a beeline for Sophia and grabs her roughly by the arm--

>   TREMONT TREMAINE
>   That new husband of yours is
>   fucking up something good!

>   MIKEY TREMAINE
>   Yeah, fucking it up!

>   TREMONT TREMAINE
>   Shut up, Mikey!

Tremont addresses the few customers that are left.

>   TREMONT TREMAINE (CONT'D)
>   Everybody get the fuck out, we're
>   closin' up!

Tremont back-hands Sophia across the face and she falls to the ground. Tremont and Mikey storm out of the diner, leaving Billy to sulk in the kitchen doorway.

Sophia gets to her feet, a hand to her face. She turns to find Billy staring at her.

>   SOPHIA DATHERS
>   What happened?

Billy shrugs. He disappears back into the kitchen.

Sophia wipes away a few tears as the last of the customers drop cash on the table and hurry out.

EXT. CHURCH - DAY

Sam cautiously approaches his cruiser. He digs into his
pocket and pulls out his car keys. The blood stained scrap of
paper he found in the Sheriff's car falls to the ground.

He picks it up, studying the partial stamp over the
signiture. He climbs into the car and drives away.

EXT. STREET - DAY

Sam's cruiser pulls up to the curb hard, the front tire jumps
up on the sidewalk. Sam climbs out, disheveled, unsteady on
his feet.

He climbs the steps into a drab two-story building with a
painted sign on the glass - "County Records Building."

INT. COUNTY RECORDS BUILDING - CONTINUOUS

The old woman, Ruth, stands across the counter from Sam, a
scowl on her face.

                    RUTH
          You look like shit.

                    DEPUTY SAM
          I need to see the deed to Clearmont
          Farms.

                    RUTH
          What's the matter, Benny rough you
          up again?

Ruth chuckles to herself.

                    SHERIFF SAM
          Benny's dead. I shot him in the
          face.

The smile on Ruth's face disappears. She clocks the blood
stains on the Sam's shirt, his changed demeanor.

                    RUTH
          Uh-what is it you wanted to see?

                    DEPUTY SAM
          Clearmont Farms.

Ruth slinks away. The other employees watch Sam. There's a
new determination behind his eyes.

Ruth returns with a folder and slides it across the counter.

Sam opens the folder. He moves his finger down the paper and lands on the name at the bottom - "Jacob Brimmel." It matches his scrap of paper.

Sam snatches up the folder and storms out--

                    RUTH
          Hey, you can't take that!

INT. DINER - KITCHEN - DAY

Billy watches Sophia clean the diner through a crack in the kitchen door.

INT. DILAPIDATED HOUSE - DAY

Jimmy is reclining with a bag of chips in his lap. Empyt beer bottles and food containers litter the table. He waches a TV show with the volume up loud.

                    MISTER FISK (O.S.)
          Turn it down...

The bag of chips flies out of Jimmy's hands and he jumps up, but Mister Fisk is behind him and slams him back into the chair, holding him in place.

                    MISTER FISK (CONT'D)
          This is disappointing, Jimmy.

                    JIMMY GRIMES
          It's not what-no, I-I was just
          resting before I go looking for
          Frankie...

                    MISTER FISK
          It's okay. I get it.

                    JIMMY GRIMES
          Uh... you do?

                    MISTER FISK
          Yeah. You're a fucking idiot. We
          gave you a chance to help us out,
          Jimmy, and in turn help yourself.
          But you chose to piss it all away.
          There are consiquences for every
          action, Jimmy... did you know that?

                         JIMMY GRIMES
                What, uh-what do you mean?

A bullet rips through the couch and tears a whole in Jimmy's
midsection, in a spray of blood.

Jimmy clutches the wound. Mister Fisk brings the gun up. He
puts it to the back of Jimmy's head and pulls the trigger,
spraying the man's face across the table and Television.

Mister fisk turns and walk into the kitchen. He looks under
the sink and pulls out a roll of plastic kitchen bags.

EXT. SIDE-STREET - DAY

Sam's cruiser is parked at a wonkey angle near the curb.

INT. SAM'S CRUISER - CONTINUOUS

Sam is slummped over the wheel asleep and snoring. His body
twitches and he jerks awake, dissoriented.

INT. DINER - DUSK

Sophia loads the last of the dishes into a plastic bin and
carries it into the kitchen.

KITCHEN--

It's dark. Sophia looks to the light switch but her hands are
full.

                         SOPHIA DATHERS
                Billy?

She moves to the sink--

                         SOPHIA DATHERS (CONT'D)
                Billy? Why am I doing your job? You
                better not be getting high...

She sets the bin down next to the sink and something crashes
into her--

Sophia is slammed to the ground with a hulking form on top of
her. She tries to fight off her assailant--

Billy Crickett. His face red, sweaty, his breathing labored,
straddles Sophia, pinning her down.

                    SOPHIA DATHERS (CONT'D)
              Billy, get off me!

Billy rips the front of her waitress dress open--

                    SOPHIA DATHERS (CONT'D)
              What the hell are you doing? Get
              off me!

                    BILLY CRICKETT
              Tremont promised me, then he took
              it back! It ain't fair!

Sophia struggles to break free. She rakes her nails across
Billy's cheek. He punches her in the face, nearly knocking
her out.

Billy puts a hand to his bleeding face.

                    BILLY CRICKETT (CONT'D)
              Bitch.

Sophia punches Billy in the balls and crawls out from under
him--

Billy grabs her ankle and Sophia falls to the ground. She
crawls away--

Billy grabs a butcher knife off the counter and follows--

                    BILLY CRICKETT (CONT'D)
              It ain't fair!

He rounds a prep tables--

Billy is smashed in the face by a cast iron skillet. He
staggers back and drops the knife, but stays on his feet.
Blood runs down his forehead from a deep gash.

                    BILLY CRICKETT (CONT'D)
              You fucking bitch!

Sophia turns and runs. Billy lunges and grabs her from
behind, pinning her against the table. With one hand he pulls
his belt open and his pants drop--

                    SOPHIA DATHERS
              Billy, stop!

A DARK SHAPE slams into Billy and he's throw sideways--

Two gunshots shatter the silence--

Sophia flips on the lights--

Billy's body is splayed out on the floor, pants around his
ankles, blood fanning out like a Rorschach test across the
floor. Sam stands over him, gun in hand.

                    DEPUTY SAM
          Oh my God... I didn't know it was
          Billy...

Billy's hand twitches. Sophia picks up the iron skillet and
stands next to Sam, looking down at her brother.

                    DEPUTY SAM (CONT'D)
          I need to call for help--

Sophia slams the skillet down on Billy's face with a
sickening crunch. She tosses it aside and turns to a shocked
Sam.

                    SOPHIA DATHERS
          He attacked me, Sam... he was going
          to have his way with me... he said
          Daddy promised it to him.

                    DEPUTY SAM
          Everyone in this town has gone mad.

Sophia steps away from Sam. She grabs one of Billy's legs and
pulls.

                    DEPUTY SAM (CONT'D)
          What are you doing?

                    SOPHIA DATHERS
          Well, we can't leave him here, and
          Daddy ain't gonna be too happy
          about this.

                    DEPUTY SAM
          Sophia, he attacked you--

                    SOPHIA DATHERS
          That won't matter to Daddy, and you
          know it. I'm done taking their
          abuse. I'm a married woman now...
          they got no power over me.

Sam grabs a leg and helps drag Billy to a freezer.

                    DEPUTY SAM
          I hate that you have to live in
          fear.

                         SOPHIA DATHERS
              This town is full of despicable
              men, Sam. It's time someone cleaned
              house.

Resolve spreads across Sam's face.

                         DEPUTY SAM
              You give me strength, Sophia. You
              make me feel like I'm capable of
              anything.

                         SOPHIA DATHERS
              You're invincible, Sam, but you
              never knew it. You just needed me
              to pull it out of you.

They kiss, then separate. Sam looks to the dead body.

                         DEPUTY SAM
              We better get him on ice, he's
              bleeding all over the floor.

Sophia smiles at Sam and opens the freezer door--

EXT. WOODS - NIGHT

Mister Fisk creeps through the dark foliage and enters a
clearing, Clearmont Farm visible across the parking lot.

A pair of headlights appear down the street and Mister Fisk
slinks back into the shadows.

INT. DINER - NIGHT

Sam and Sophia sit in a booth drinking coffee. Several wafers
are laid out on the table along with the folder from the
County.

                         DEPUTY SAM
              I believe they put the property
              under Sheriff Brimmel's name as
              insurance to keep him in line. The
              Sheriff wasn't crooked, he was on
              to them. I know they killed him,
              but I'll need proof...

Sam is out of his seat and pacing, angry.

                    DEPUTY SAM (CONT'D)
          This whole thing was orchestrated,
          and Tremont and my Daddy have been
          pulling the strings. With Frankie
          back they needed the Sheriff gone
          and me in the hot seat, because
          they figured they could control me.

                    SOPHIA DATHERS
          They were wrong, Sam.

Sam stops. Sophia takes his hand.

                    SOPHIA DATHERS (CONT'D)
          The Sheriff was like a father to
          you... and he loved you like a son.
          They knew that and they took it all
          away, for what... money? You can't
          abide their depravity, Sam.

Sam kneels beside her.

                    DEPUTY SAM
          I'm so angry, Sophia, I feel like
          it's gonna consume me, like I'm
          burning up from the inside... there
          are things I've set my mind to
          doing... I just don't want you to
          think less of me. I wan't you to be
          able to love me freely, without
          reservation...

Sophia brushes her fingers through Sam's hair and kisses him
gently on the lips. She places his campaign hat on his head.

                    SOPHIA DATHERS
          Show them what you're made of, Sam.
          Nothing can change the way I feel
          about you. And I know the Sheriff
          would be proud.

Sam stands.

                    DEPUTY SAM
          Then I'll see justice served.

Sam walks away.

EXT. CLEARMAONT FARM - NIGHT

A pickup truck pulls into the lot and two scruffy men climb
out and walk to the door. SULLY, 32, and VERN, 48.

                    SULLY
          Man, I was havin' dinner with my
          old lady at the Frosty Freeze. This
          better be important.

                    VERN
          That's nice. How's yer Mamma doin'?

                    SULLY
          No, I was with my wife. My wife is
          my old lady, you idiot.

Sully goes to punch the code in the wall keypad--

                    VERN
          How the fuck do I know who yer old
          lady is...

A gun is jammed into the back of Sully's head.

                    MISTER FISK
          No sudden moves, boys.

                    VERN
          Okay, mister, we ain't lookin' to
          get shot.

                    MISTER FISK
          Good, then all you got to do is
          give me the alarm code.

Sully eyes Mister Fisk.

                    SULLY
          Jesus, yer big...

                    MISTER FISK
          What's the code?

                    VERN
          You know I can't tell you that.

Mister Fisk grabs Vern by the collar and slams him down on
the ground, shoving the gun under his chin--

                    MISTER FISK
          Then you're of no use to me.

Mister Fisk pulls the trigger and the top of Vern's head is
blown open. Sully screams--

Mister Fisk clamps his hand over Sully's mouth and pins him
against the building.

                        MISTER FISK (CONT'D)
              What's the code?

Sully mumbles something incoherent and Mister Fisk removes
his hand.

                        SULLY
              Please, I got an old lady-a wife...
              She's waitin' on me at the--

Mister Fisk shoves the gun under his chin.

                        MISTER FISK
              Tell me the code.

                        SULLY
              And then you'll let me go?

                        MISTER FISK
              The code.

                        SULLY
              Okay, okay, it's ten-twenty-eight.

Mister Fisk puts in the code and the door clicks open.

                        MISTER FISK
              I appreciate you not lyin' to me.

                        SULLY
              So... you're gonna let me go,
              right?

Mister Fisk jerks Sully away from the wall and pulls the
trigger, putting a bullet in his forehead.

                        MISTER FISK
              No.

Mister Fisk grabs Sully and Vern by the ankles and drags them
towards the woods.

INT. CHURCH - OFFICE - NIGHT

Tremont and Frankie help Father Janis clean up the mess.
Mikey stands of to the side on his phone.

                        TREMONT TREMAINE
              Hey, dummy, you gonna help here?

Mikey slides the phone back into his pocket.

                    MIKEY TREMAINE
          Billy ain't answerin.' I think he's
          sore we didn't bring him?

Tremont grumbles.

                    TREMONT TREMAINE
          Jesus Christ, you idiot's are gonna
          be the death of me...

                    FATHER JANIS
          Not that I don't enjoy your moronic
          squabbles, but what the fuck are we
          gonna do about Sam?

                    TREMONT TREMAINE
          This is why I had him and Sophia
          hitched. He's family know... Sam
          just needs a little motivation to
          see things in the right light...
              (to Mikey)
          Go pick up Sophia and bring her to
          the farm. She's all the motivation
          we need.

Mikey sulks.

                    MIKEY TREMAINE
          Fine, gimmie the keys.

                    TREMONT TREMAINE
          It's four fucking blocks, walk.

Mikey sighs, exasperated.

                    TREMONT TREMAINE (CONT'D)
          Meet us at the Farm. You can take
          Billy's truck.

                    MIKEY TREMAINE
              (mumbles)
          His truck smells like balls.

Mikey shuffles away, and the two men go about packing up.

                    FATHER JANIS
          Look, I don't know how Sam came
          upon this sudden streak of good
          luck, but right now that boy could
          shit in a swinging bucket. We need
          to take this serious. We need to
          take precautions.

Tremont nods in agreement.

INT. SAM'S CRUISER - NIGHT

Sam drives, determined. He pulls his phone out and makes a call, the sound coming through the car's speakers.

After several rings there's an answer--

                    WARDEN KEPLER
          Warden Kepler.

                    DEPUTY SAM
          Warden, this is Deputy Sam Dathers.
          I'm hoping that you can clear
          something up for me.

There's a hesitation on the line.

                    WARDEN KEPLER
          Uh... yes, what can I do for you,
          Deputy.

                    DEPUTY SAM
          You can explain to me why my
          brother Frankie was released after
          serving three years of an eighteen
          year sentance.

                    WARDEN KEPLER
          I don't care for your tone, Deputy.
          I'll not be interigated--

                    DEPUTY SAM
          I don't know what's been going on
          up there, Warden, but I'm gonna get
          to the bottom of it. I can promise
          you that.

                    WARDEN KEPLER
          Now you listen to me you little
          shit--

Sam hangs up the phone.

EXT. CLEARMONT FARM - NIGHT

Tremont's truck and Frankie's muscle-car pull into the empty parking lot and they all climb out.

                    TREMONT TREMAINE
          Where the fuck are Sully and Vern?
          They should've had the place open
          by now... Fucking worthless shits.

                    FRANKIE DATHERS
          You get what you pay for with these
          fuckin' yokels.

                    TREMONT TREMAINE
          Shut up, Frankie. You were born in
          this town too.

                    FRANKIE DATHERS
          You know, you better start showin'
          me some goddamn respect, Tremont. I
          don't like the way you talk to me.

                    TREMONT TREMAINE
          We got bigger fish to fry than your
          inflated fuckin' ego, Frankie.

                    FATHER JANIS
          Can you two stop stepping on your
          dicks and get on with this.

They move to the side door and Tremont punches the code into
the keypad.

                    TREMONT TREMAINE
          I'm just saying, everything started
          going to shit the minute you came
          back to town.

Tremont and the Father walk inside.

                    FRANKIE DATHERS
          Fuck you, Tremont.

Frankie follows.

EXT. DINER - NIGHT

Mikey walks through the parking lot.

INT. DINER - CONTINUOUS

The place is dark, quiet. Mikey enters and heads to the
kitchen--

KITCHEN

Mikey stands frozen in the doorway, taking in the scene--

Stacks of frozen meats are pilled up on the floor and Billy's
body is stuffed into the freezer with the lid still open.

Sophia-having changed clothes, is mopping up a large blood stain on the floor.

                    MIKEY TREMAINE
          What the holy shit?

Startled, Sophia drops the mop handle. Mikey rushes to the freezer and stares down at his friends dead body--

                    MIKEY TREMAINE (CONT'D)
          What the holy shit?!

                    SOPHIA DATHERS
          He attacked me... the bastard was
          trying to rape me!

                    MIKEY TREMAINE
          Stupid son of a bitch, we told him
          not to...

Sophia's eyes darken.

                    SOPHIA DATHERS
          You knew of his intensions?

                    MIKEY TREMAINE
          Well, we told him not to.

                    SOPHIA DATHERS
          And you and Daddy left me here
          alone with him?!

Mikey leans in and inspects the wounds--

                    MIKEY TREMAINE
          He was shot--

Sophia snatches the iron skillet from the counter and smashes Mikey in the side of the head--

Mikey careens into a shelving unit and crumples to the ground. Sophia slams the lid on the freezer and walks out of the kitchen--

DINNING AREA

Sophia steps out of the kitchen and Mikey is behind her. He lunges--

Sophia spins. She slams the skillet into Mikey's forehead and he staggers back, but stays on his feet.

                    MIKEY TREMAINE (CONT'D)
          Ow, fuck...

Mikey rubs his forehead. He's bleeding from a gash on the side of his head.

> MIKEY TREMAINE (CONT'D)
> You bitch... you never did like
> Billy... or me!

> SOPHIA DATHERS
> Fuck you, Mikey, you did nothing
> but treat me like shit my entire
> life, and you stood by when Daddy
> was beatin' on me. You did nothing!
> Don't you dare try and turn this
> around on me.

Mikey laughs.

> MIKEY TREMAINE
> Oh man, Daddy's gonna skin you
> alive. When he finds out that Sam
> fuckin'... whoah...

Mikey sways, grabs hold of the countertop to stabilize himself.

> MIKEY TREMAINE (CONT'D)
> Feelin' a little woozy...

He looks to Sophia--

> MIKEY TREMAINE (CONT'D)
> Well don't just stand there... get
> some goddamn ice for my head.

Sophia walks up, swings the skillet right into Mikey's crotch, and watches him collapses with a whimper.

She pulls his cell phone out of his pocket, drops it on the floor, and smashes it with the skillet.

> SOPHIA DATHERS
> Now, I'm gonna go help my husband
> get some well deserved retribution.

> MIKEY TREMAINE
> (Squeaks)
> Bitch...

Sophia steps over him--

INT. JAILHOUSE - NIGHT

Sam stands at his desk. He loads his antique Colt pistol and slides in into the back of his waistband.

He unlocks the middle drawer and pulls out Sheriff Brimmel's gold badge. He holds it in his hand--

Resolved, Sam unpins his Deputy badge and pins the Sheriff's star on his chest.

EXT. DINER - NIGHT

Sophia opens the truck door and tosses the skillet onto the seat. She steps up on the sideboard--

She's grabbed from behind and yanked down. Mikey spins her around and slams her head into the side of the truck and she crumples.

INT. JAILHOUSE - NIGHT

Sam locks his desk drawer and pulls out his cellphone. He tries Sophia's number but it goes straight to voicemail.

INT. BILLY'S TRUCK - NIGHT

Mikey and Sophia drive in sullen silence, her hands duct-taped in front of her. She Turns to her brother--

    MIKEY TREMAINE   SOPHIA DATHERS
I can't believe you'd do that   You better let me go, Mikey!
to him!

                      SOPHIA DATHERS (CONT'D)
                Billy attacked me, what choice did
                Sam have?

                      MICKEY TREMAINE
                You didn't have to cave his fucking
                face in! He might'a lived!

                      SOPHIA DATHERS
                I won't have men defining my life
                anymore.

They retreat back into silence...

                      SOPHIA TREMAINE
                It smells like balls in here.

EXT. DINER - NIGHT

Sam's cruiser tears into the parking lot and screeches to a
halt. Sam is on the move--

INT. DINER - CONTINUOUS

Sam plows through the door and rushes inside. He stops dead
in his tracks at a splash of blood on the dinning-room floor.

                    SHERIFF SAM
          Sophia?!

Sam runs into the kitchen--

KITCHEN

Empty. Sam rushes out the door--

INT. BILLY'S TRUCK - NIGHT

Sophia watches Mikey drive, her eyes narrow slits of hate

                    SOPHIA DATHERS
          If you hurt my husband, I will bash
          your stupid face in.

Mikey throws her a wary glance.

                    MIKEY TREMAINE
          You've changed.

EXT. ROAD - NIGHT

Sam's cruiser fishtails around a corner and pulls onto the
road. He hits the gas and is flying--

INT. BILLY'S TRUCK - CONTINUOUS

Mikey checks the rearview mirror-- there's a car coming up on
them fast.

                    MIKEY TREMAINE
          What the fuck?

INT. SAM'S CRUISER - CONTINUOUS

Sam switches his spinners on, painting the night in blue and
red. Mikey doesn't slow.

INT. BILLY'S TRUCK - CONTINUOUS

Mickey flips the rearview mirror up to get the blinding lights out of his eyes.

                    SOPHIA DATHERS
              Pull over and let Sam explain
              himself.

                    MIKEY TREMAINE
              Fuck him... and fuck you.

Sam's cruiser moves up along side Mikey, but he cuts him off. Sam drops behind the pickup, then accelerates to pulls up along the passenger side--

                                        SMASH CUT TO:

INT. SHERIFF BRIMMEL'S CRUISER - NIGHT

Sheriff Brimmel's face is cold steel, eyes burning as he pulls along side Billy's truck--

INT. SAM'S CRUISER - BACK TO PRESENT - NIGHT

Sam looks up to Sophia in the passenger seat. She frantically motions for him to look ahead--

They're coming up on a sharpe curve in the road. A sign reads Parker Curve--

                    SHERIFF SAM
              Oh crap....

The pickup slams into the cruiser. Sam crushes the brakes--

                                        SMASH CUT TO:

INT. SHERIFF BRIMMEL'S CRUISER - NIGHT

Sheriff Brimmel hits the brakes and careens off the road, slamming into a tree--

INT. SAM'S CRUISER - BACK TO PRESENT - NIGHT

Sam skids off the road and slams into the tree--

INT. BILLY'S TRUCK - CONTINUOUS

Sophia strains to see out the back window as the pickup
speeds away.

                    SOPHIA DATHERS
              You son of a bitch! You better pray
              Sam's okay.

Mikey shoots her a frightened look--

INT. SAM'S CRUISER - CONTINUOUS

The front end of the cruiser is smashed into the tree. Sam is
dazed, staring at the wreckage--

                                        SMASH CUT TO:

EXT. PARKER CURVE - FLASHBACK - NIGHT

The Sheriff's car is mangled, wraped around a tree.

Billy's pickup is parked at the side of the road--

The passenger door pops open and a SHADOWY FIGURE slides out.
The figure approaches the cruiser and steps into the bright
light of the cruisers headlights--

Frankie Dathers stares down at the Sheriff's bloody face. His
body tangled in the wreckage, breathing wet and labopred.

Frankie rips the door open and inspects the damage. There's a
piece of paper on the floor by the Sheriff's feet. Frankie
reaches in and pulls it out--

The Sheriff grabs it, startling Frakie.

Frankie rips it free, a piece tearing off in the Sheriff's
fist.

Frankie places a hand on the gun in his waistbnand--

The Sheriff has stopped breathing, his dead eyes stare back.

Frankie walks away and the ripped piece of paper falls out of
the Sheriff's lifeless hand--

INT. SAM'S CRUISER - BACK TO PRESENT - NIGHT

Sam wipes blood and sweat out of his eyes. The picture of
Sheriff Brimmel taped to his dash stares back at him.

He turns the key and the engine whines and clanks, finally
sputtering to life.

EXT. CLEARMONT FARMS - NIGHT

The pickup pulls into the parking lot and Mikey climbs out.
The side door of the barn opens and Tremont steps outside--

                    TREMONT TREMAINE
          What took you so long?

Grim faced, Mikey pulls the passenger door open and roughly
yanks Sophia out.

                    TREMONT TREMAINE (CONT'D)
          What the hell's going on, Mikey?

Sophia stares daggers at her father as Mikey drags her
towards the building.

                    MIKEY TREMAINE
          They killed Billy.

INT. SAM'S CRUISER - CONTINUOUS

The cruiser limps slowly along the dark road, headlights
pointing in different directions. Sam's phone rings--

He pulls it out of his pocket-- the caller I.D. reads -
"Sophia." He answers--

                    SHERIFF SAM
          Sophia, thank God--

INT. BARN - CONTINUOUS

Sophia is slumped over in a chair, face bloody, hands still
taped. Tremont has the phone to his ear. He's pacing--

                    TREMONT TREMAINE
          You son of a bitch, you killed
          Billy!

INT. SAM'S CRUISER - CONTINUOUS

Sam clutches the phone.

                    SHERIFF SAM
          If you hurt her--

INT. BARN - CONTINUOUS

Tremont stops pacing. Mikey grabs the back of Sophia's chair and drags her away.

                    TREMONT TREMAINE
          I suggest you follow my
          instructions, before things take a
          very dark turn for you...

INT. BARN - 2ND LEVEL - CONTINUOUS

Mister Fisk hides amongst the clutter of a storage platform in the rafters. He watches through the wide slats in the wood floor.

EXT. CLEARMONT FARM - NIGHT

Sam's cruiser limps into the parking lot and stops. He climbs out of the car, unbuckles his gun belt and untucks his shirt.

INT. BARN - CONTINUOUS

Father Janis and Tremont pack duffle bags full of drugs. Frankie leafs through a girlie magazine.

                    TREMONT TREMAINE
          If this goes south--

                    FRANKIE DATHERS
          It's not gonna go south cuz we got
          Sophia... as long as you don't lose
          your shit.

                    TREMONT TREMAINE
          I'm not promising anything. I'm
          leaning towards killing Sam.

                    FRANKIE DATHERS
          Billy was tryin' to diddle her. I
          don't think you can place the blame
          square on Sam for this one.

                    FATHER JANIS
          You're not killin' Sam! There's
          been enough blood shed already. You
          want this place crawlin' with
          county men?

                    TREMONT TREMAINE
          I'm undicided...

Frankie throws a look to his father.

BACK ROOM

Mickey stands at the door trying to hear what's going on.

> SOPHIA DATHERS
> (whispers)
> Mikey... Mikey...

He turns--

> MIKEY TREMAINE
> Would you stop--

Sophia kicks him in the balls and he collapses to the floor.
She pulls his truck keys out of his pocket.

BARN

Frankie gets up from his chair.

> FRANKIE DATHERS
> You guys are fucking amateurs, you
> know that? It's no wonder the
> Sheriff figured you out...

> FATHER JANIS
> We're all on edge here, boy, don't
> push things.

> FRANKIE DATHERS
> You left a Goddamn paper trail...
> and neither of you had the balls to
> take care of him, so that fell to
> me... once again.

> SHERRIF SAM (O.S.)
> You son of a bitch...

All three men look up and freeze--

Sam steps out of the shadows, gun belt in hand, shaking with
rage.

> FRANKIE DATHERS
> Fuck.

Frankie trains his gun on Sam.

> SHERIFF SAM
> You killed the Sheriff.

                    TREMONT TREMAINE
              You killed Billy!

                    SHERIFF SAM
              He attacked your daughter!

Father Janis tries to ease the tension. He steps close to
Sam.

                    FATHER JANIS
              Okay now, remember our agreement,
              we just want to talk. Let's all
              calm down and think about what
              we're tryin' to build here, not
              what we've lost along the way...

                    SHERIFF SAM
              I'm not here to build anything with
              you.

                    TREMONT TREMAINE
              You just remember that I've got
              Sophia, so I suggest you start
              playing ball--

Sam punches Father Janis in the face, and the Father hits the
ground hard--

                    FATHER JANIS
              What the fuck?

                    SHERIFF SAM
              I'm done taking orders from any of
              you--

Sam is hit from behind and he crumples to the ground--

Mikey stands over him, one hand clutching his crotch, the
other a chair leg.

                    MIKEY TREMAINE
              Sophia got away.

                    TREMONT TREMAINE
              Goddammit, Mikey, you had one job!

                    MIKEY TREMAINE
              I don't mind tellin' you, I'm
              scared 'ah her. She's changed--

Mikey's head jerks sideways, and he collapses. Sophia steps
out of the shadows, iron skillet in hand.

                    TREMONT TREMAINE
               Jesus Christ, are you tryin' to
               kill him too?

Sophia drops the skillet and pulls Sam's gun from his fallen
gun belt.

Frankie's gun is on Sophia.

                    FRANKIE DATHERS
               You look good, Sophia. It's been a
               while.

                    SOPHIA DATHERS
               Fuck you, Frankie. Put the gun
               down, or I'll shoot you in the
               balls.

                    TREMONT TREMAINE
               What the hell's gotten into you,
               Sophia? Have you lost your goddamn
               mind? Put the gun down!

                    SOPHIA DATHERS
               Did you know he raped me when I was
               sixteen?

Tremont moves closer.

                    TREMONT TREMAINE
               Sophia, you're hysterical, you need
               to calm down. He was a teenager,
               men have urges at that age... It's
               nature--

Sophia swings the gun around on Tremont.

                    SOPHIA DATHERS
               Are you kidding me, you knew?

                    TREMONT TREMAINE
               I mean, we didn't talk about it,
               but...

                    SOPHIA DATHERS
               I can't believe this.

Tremont takes another step closer.

                    TREMONT TREMAINE
               Put the gun down, Sophia, we can
               still work all this out.

                    SOPHIA DATHERS
          You're not hurting my Sam. He
          defended me. He protected me from
          Billy, which is more than you've
          ever done.

Tremont steps closer. He grabs Sophia's wrist and lands a
solid punch to her face, knocking her to the ground. The gun
clatters to the floor.

STORAGE LOFT--

Mister Fisk watches from his perch, a wicked smile on his
face.

                    MISTER FISK
          Idiots.

MAIN FLOOR--

Mikey and Father Janis are on their feet. Sam sits up--

                    SHERIFF SAM
               (moans)
          Who hit me?

Mikey grabs the fallen gun and stands over Sophia. He rubs
his eyes--

                    MICKEY TREMAINE
          Goddamnit, Sophia, I'm gonna be
          permanently crosseyed, and I ain't
          never gonna be able to have kids!
          Stop hitting me with that
          fucking... Whoah...

Mikey sways.

                    SOPHIA DATHERS
          Idiot.

                    SHERIFF SAM
          Don't you touch her, Mikey. I'm the
          one who shot Billy.

                    MICKEY TREMAINE
          Oh, I'm gonna get to you... don't
          you worry... you just won't go
          away... you're like a goddamn hound
          on the scent of an oily rag--

Sam scoots across the floor and launches a boot into Mikey's
crotch. Mikey screams, fires his gun into the air, and
collapses in a heap--

There's a loud thud from above, a splintering of old wood, and a hulking form drops down from the rafters to land squarely on top of Sam.

> TREMONT TREMAINE
> Who the hell is this?

> FRANKIE DATHERS
> Well, fuck me... that's Mister
> Fisk. He's Warden Kepler's right
> hand goon.

> TREMONT TREMAINE
> I told you you were pushing the
> Warden too hard.

Frankie scratches his head.

> FRANKIE DATHERS
> Yeah, you may have been right about
> that one.

Mister Fisk stirs, blood seeping from a bullet wound in his shoulder. He rolls off of Sam.

> TREMONT TREMAINE
> Jesus, he's big.

Mister Fisk grabs Frankie's ankle and pulls his feet out from under him. The gun flies out of his hand and he hits his head on the ground when he falls--

Tremont jumps on Mister Fisk's back and tries to get him in a choke hold--

Sam scrambles to his feet. He punches his father in the face and stands over him. He pulls out his cuffs--

> SHERIFF SAM
> You're under arrest for your part
> in the murder of Sheriff Brimmel,
> drug running, kidnapping my wife,
> and the attempted murder of my
> Mamma!

Mister Fisk is spinning in circles and crashing into everything, trying to get Tremont off his back--

Sam drags Father Janis to a work table and handcuffs him to it--

> FATHER JANIS
> Christ, boy, I didn't touch yer
> mother, you idiot!

Mister Fisk and Tremont plow into Sam and they all fall in a heap--

Tremont spots Mister Fisk's gun and dives for it. Mister Fisk gets to his feet and is smashed in the face with a metal wafer tray by Frankie. The big man stumbles back--

Tremont fires two shots and Mister Fisk drops to the ground. Tremont turns his gun on Sam--

                    TREMONT TREMAINE
          Get up, Sam.

Sam stands.

                    TREMONT TREMAINE (CONT'D)
          I drugged your mother.

          FATHER JANIS   FRANKIE DATHERS
What the fuck, Tremont!   You son of a bitch!

                    TREMONT TREMAINE
          Oh for god's sake, she doesn't even
          know her own name. She was a
          distraction for Sam.

                    SHERIFF SAM
          She's my Mother!

                    TREMONT TREMAINE
          Oh fuck off, Sam! Everything's a
          distraction for you. The Sheriff
          dying, your Mamma, your fucking toy
          soldiers...

Mikey lets out a loud moan and lurches to his feet, gripping his balls. He snatches a pair of scissors off a work station--

                    MIKEY TREMAINE
          You're not gonna hit me with that
          fucking skillet again--

Mikey charges at Sophia, crazed, scissors over his head--

Sam reaches under his shirt, pulls the Colt pistol out of his waistband, and shoots Mikey--

Mikey stumbles and falls face-first on the ground--

Tremont is frozen in shock. Sophia moves to Mikey and rolls him over--

The scissors are buried to the handle in his chest.

                    SOPHIA DATHERS
            Oh, that's not good...

Tremont's face flips from shock to rage. he raises his gun
and pulls the trigger--

Sophia leaps in front of Sam--

The bullet hits the skillet, ricochets off it, and hits
Frankie in the calf. He screams and falls--

Sam shoots Tremont, and the man drops, clutching his stomach.

                    SHERIFF SAM
            You're all going to jail.

                    FATHER JANIS
            This is a mistake, Son--

                    SHERIFF SAM
            I'm not your son! I gave you up the
            day you beat my Mamma's head in.

                    FATHER JANIS
            I'm your goddamn father, you'll do
            as your told!

Sam points to his shiny gold star.

                    SHERIFF SAM
            I'm the Goddamned Sheriff now.
            You're nothing but a lying drug
            dealing murderer.

Tremont is lying prone, hands over his wound, oozing blood
from his abdomen. Sophia moves to him and puts a hand on top
of his.

Frankie watches them from the floor, clutching his leg. He
spots his gun lying nearby.

                    TREMONT TREMAINE
            I'm gut shot, Sophia... I need your
            help... I need an ambulance...

Sophia pushes down on Tremont's hands.

                    TREMONT TREMAINE (CONT'D)
            Aaaahhh! What the Hell's wrong with
            you? You've lost your Goddamn mind,
            girl.

                    SOPHIA DATHERS
            No Daddy... I woke up.

                  TREMONT TREMAINE
            (pleading)
        Help me... please... call for help.

Sophia pulls his cell phone from his pocket and tosses it on
his chest.

                  SOPHIA DATHERS
        Call 'em yourself.

She stands and looks at the carnage.

                  SOPHIA DATHERS (CONT'D)
        Hey... where's the big guy?

                  SHERIFF SAM
    Damn.

Frankie awkwardly climbs to his feet and grabs Sophia from
behind, shoving his gun into her side.

                  FRANKIE DATHERS
        Sammy--

Sam spins, and his pistol comes up.

                  FRANKIE DATHERS (CONT'D)
        Now, we both know yer not gonna
        shoot me as long as I've got yer
        precious Sophia.

Sam lowers his weapon.

                  FRANKIE DATHERS (CONT'D)
        All the way down, Sam.

Sam puts the gun on the ground.

                  FRANKIE DATHERS (CONT'D)
        Well, you have royally fucked
        things up for me, Sammy. We had a
        nice family business goin' here. No
        one was askin' you to take part,
        all you had to do was look the
        other way.

                  SHERIFF SAM
        You're selling drugs out of the
        church. I'm not looking the other
        way. I did it when our Daddy broke
        Mamma's skull open, but I'm done
        being intimidated by you two. I'm
        shutting it down. All of it.

Sophia squirms and Frankie tightens his grip.

                    FRANKIE DATHERS
          You've changed, Sammy, I'll give
          you that. I guess marriage agrees
          with you--

Frankie licks Sophia's neck. She cringes. Sam's blood boils.
He takes a step closer--

                    FRANKIE DATHERS (CONT'D)
          Nope. Don't do that, Sammy. You
          wouldn't want somethin' to happen
          to your pretty little bride.

                    SOPHIA DATHERS
          If you think you're taking me with
          you, you should know. The second
          you close your eyes, or turn your
          back on me, I'm gonna rip off your
          face, shove it down your throat,
          and watch you choke to death on
          youre ugliness.

                    FRANKIE DATHERS
          Wow, that's really dark...

Sam walks over to his gun and slowly bends down to pick it
up.

                    FRANKIE DATHERS (CONT'D)
          Don't do it, Sammy.

Sam stands, gun in hand.

                    SOPHIA DATHERS
          He's not gonna just let you walk
          outta here.

                    FRANKIE DATHERS
          No, I don't suppose he is... but he
          can't save you and catch me. Let's
          see what's more important to him--

Frankie pushes Sophia away from him. He fires one shot. The
bullet hits her in the leg and she falls--

                    SHERIFF SAM
          Sophia!

Frankie bolts into the shadows and Sam runs to Sophia.

EXT. BARN - CONTINUOUS

Frankie bursts through the side door and runs to his car. He
fumbles for his keys. A hulking figure steps up behind him-

                    MISTER FISK
          Toss the gun and turn around,
          Frankie.

Frankie sighs. He tosses the gun and turns.

INT. BARN - CONTINUOUS

Sam puts pressure on Sophia's leg. She's unfazed.

                    SOPHIA DATHERS
          Sam, it's just a flesh wound. Go
          after Frankie.

                    SHERIFF SAM
          No, I'm not leaving your side till
          I know you're all right.

She puts a hand to his face.

                    SOPHIA DATHERS
          Sam, you chose me. I'm fine. Go do
          your job... the Sheriff's watching.

Sam kisses her.

                    SHERIFF SAM
          I love you, Sophia Dathers.

                    SOPHIA DATHERS
          I love you, Sheriff Dathers.

Sam boltss for the door.

EXT. BARN - CONTINUOUS

Frankie and Mister Fisk stand facing each other.

                    MISTER FISK
          Now the keys. Aim for the woods.

Frankie throws the keys into the woods.

                         MISTER FISK (CONT'D)
                    Hope you're happy, Frankie. Now I
                    have to kill your brother and his
                    wife too. And I don't enjoy killing
                    women... especially pretty ones.

                         FRANKIE DATHERS
                    I feel you, big man. Now, what's it
                    gonna take to work out a deal
                    here...

The side door bursts open and Sam runs out, pistol raised. He
freezes.

Mister Fisk grabs Frankie and uses him as a shield.

                         SHERIFF SAM
                    You've lost your way, Mister Fisk.
                    You're supposed to be on the side
                    of law and order.

                         MISTER FISK
                    I'm affraid the other side pays
                    better.

                         FRANKIE DATHERS
                    And there's prostitutes.

Mister Fisk slaps Frankie upside his head.

                         MISTER FISK
                    Shut up.

Mister Fisk pushes Frankie forward. They slowly walk towards
Sam.

                         MISTER FISK (CONT'D)
                    Let's take this inside and talk
                    about what happens next. I believe
                    we can come to an arrangement.

                         FRANKIE DATHERS
                    He's gonna kill us, Sam... Sophia
                    too.

Sam looks into Mister Fisk's eyes. The big man doesn't bother
denying it.

Both men fire. Mister Fisk misses. Sam's bullet rips through
Mister Fisk's eye and blows a hole in the back of his head.
The big man toples--

Frankie turns and runs into the woods, calling out--

                    FRANKIE DATHERS
          Thanks little brother!

                    SHERIFF SAM
          Damn.

Sam watches him get swallowed up by the woods as sirens wail
and an ambulance and fire truck pull into the parking lot.

TITLE CARD: SEVERAL MONTHS LATER

INT. BIKINI BAR - NIGHT

Frankie sits at a small table in the corner of the seedy room
with several shot glasses in front of him. A single dancer
half-heartedly works the pole on a small stage.

Sam walk through the front door. He spots Frankie and makes
his way to the table, sitting opposite him. He leaves his hat
on.

Frankie frowns.

                    FRANKIE DATHERS
          Ain't you gonna take your stupid
          hat off?

                    SHERIFF SAM
          No. I won't be here long.

                    FRANKIE DATHERS
          How'd you find me?

                    SHERIFF SAM
          You beat up a prostitute.

                    FRANKIE DATHERS
          Fair enough.

Frankie pulls out his gun and lays it on the table, barrel
facing Sam.

                    FRANKIE DATHERS (CONT'D)
          Heard Tremont's on his ass,
          shittin' in a bag for the rest of
          his days... never did like that son
          of a bitch.

Frankie throws back another shot.

                    FRANKIE DATHERS (CONT'D)
          You know, I bet good money that
          we'd break you, and you'd fall into
          line.

Sam slowly pulls his Colt pistol out and lays it on the
table, barrel facing Frankie.

                    SHERIFF SAM
          Well, I guess you lost that bet.

Frankie shrugs.

                    FRANKIE DATHERS
          Yes and no, on account 'ah you
          shootin' Benny in the face, so... I
          don't have to pay up. I feel like
          that's a win.

Frankie grabs another shot and holds it up for a toast.

                    FRANKIE DATHERS (CONT'D)
          I appreciate what you did back at
          the farm, with Fisk. If he'd of
          killed me, there'd be no one left
          to sing my virtues, seein' as how
          you put the Preacher in jail.

                    SHERIFF SAM
          I didn't do it for you.

                    FRANKIE DATHERS
          No, I don't suppose you did.

Frankie throws back the shot and slams the glass down.

                    FRANKIE DATHERS (CONT'D)
          Now, off you go, Sammy. Flitter
          away into the sunset... I'm gonna
          cut you some slack cuz at the end
          of the day we're still family, and
          that's something you never offered
          me...

Sam slowly pulls out his handcuffs and slides them across the
table.

                    SHERIFF SAM
          Here's your slack, Frankie. I'm
          offering you a choice... since
          we're family.

                    FRANKIE DATHERS
          You know what? I don't like this
          new version of you.

Sam gives him the hint of a smirk.

                    FRANKIE DATHERS (CONT'D)
          Fuck you. We made you the Sheriff.

Sam's smirk hardens into a cold stare.

                    SHERIFF SAM
          I earned this star... and you
          killed the Sheriff... he was a good
          man. I won't let that go.

                    FRANKIE DATHERS
          Oh, boo-hoo, Sammy. Grow up. Good
          people die every day. You may have
          grown some little baby balls, but
          we both know that deep down you're
          still--

Sam's gun barks, and a bullet rips through Frankie's
shoulder, throwing him backward. He hits the ground hard.

Sam holsters his pistol as he stands and tucks Frankie's gun
into his waistband. He stands over his brother.

                    FRANKIE DATHERS (CONT'D)
          You fucker, you shot me...

                    SHERIFF SAM
          You shot my wife.

Sam grabs Frankie by the collar and drags him across the
floor--

TITTLE CARD: ONE MONTH LATER

INT. SHALTON PRISON - DAY

Sam escorts Frankie-in his prison jumpsuit and arm sling,
down a long row of cells. They pass several familiar faces,
all watching them walk by--

Tremont, in a wheel chair, eyes burning with hate, Father
Janis Dathers, scowling, and Warden Kepler, fearfully pressed
into the corner of his cell.

Sam pushes Frankie into the next open cell and closes the
door. Father Janis steps to the bars of his cell--

                    FATHER JANIS
          You got your whole family locked
          up. I hope you're good and Goddamn
          happy with yourself, Sam.

                    SHERIFF SAM
          You put yourself behind those bars,
          old man... you all did.

Sam walks away with his head held high.

EXT. SHALTON PRISON - DAY

Sam steps through the guard gate. Sophia is waiting by Sam's
cruiser, with his mother in the back seat. She gives Sam a
hug.

                    SOPHIA DATHERS
          Sheriff Brimmel would be so proud
          of you, Sam.

Sam smiles.

                    SHERIFF SAM
          You know... I think you're right.

Sam looks to his mother.

                    SHERRIF SAM
          How about I take my two favorite
          ladies to lunch?

Sam opens Sophia's door and helps her into the car. He walks
around the car and climbs in.

                    SOPHIA DATHERS
          I believe you've found your
          calling, Sheriff Dathers.

Sam smiles and fires up the engine.

                    SHERRIF SAM
          I believe I have.

He puts the car in gear and drives off.

                                        THE END.

Made in the USA
Monee, IL
04 September 2021

77322739R00066